A Taste of
Sauvignon

Books by Heather Heyford

A Taste of Sauvignon
A Taste of Merlot
A Taste of Chardonnay

A Taste of Sauvignon

The Napa Wine Heiresses

HEATHER HEYFORD

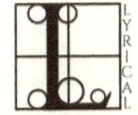

LYRICAL PRESS
Kensington Publishing Corp.
www.kensingtonbooks.com

LYRICAL PRESS BOOKS are published by

Kensington Publishing Corp.
119 West 40th Street
New York, NY 10018

All Kensington titles, imprints, and distributed lines are available at special quantity discounts for bulk purchases for sales promotion, premiums, fund-raising, educational, or institutional use.

Special book excerpts or customized printings can also be created to fit specific needs. For details, write or phone the office of the Kensington Special Sales Manager: Kensington Publishing Corp., 119 West 40th Street, New York, NY 10018. Attn. Special Sales Department. Phone: 1-800-221-2647.

Lyrical and the L logo are trademarks of Kensington Publishing Corp.

First Electronic Edition: April 2015
eISBN-13: 978-1-60183-361-7
eISBN-10: 1-60183-361-X

First Print Edition: April 2015
ISBN-13: 978-1-60183-365-5
ISBN-10: 1-60183-365-2

Printed in the United States of America

This book is dedicated to all those with the courage to pursue their dreams.

ACKNOWLEDGMENTS

Thank you to my editor, Esi Sogah, and my agent, Sarah E. Younger for your belief, support, and guidance.

To Art, for your enthusiasm.

To my tribe of writer friends, especially The Four Winds.

And to my readers. I'm moved by your acceptance and generosity. Thank you and stay in touch at heatherheyford.com.

Chapter 1

Sauvignon St. Pierre pulled the first little black dress from the left side of the rod in her precision-tuned walk-in closet. Later that evening, she would replace it on its padded hanger and hang it to the far right. And so on for the next two months, until today's dress came back into rotation.

From neat rows of acrylic boxes, each with a photo of its contents taped onto the end, she picked out a pair of two-and-a-half-inch black pumps.

The only aspect of her workday routine that couldn't be pre-arranged was which of her myriad fragrances to wear. Not even *she* could plan her mood ahead of time.

This morning, her hand hovered over flagons of every shape and pastel hue before landing on Maman's special rose perfume . . . for luck.

Savvy had made a calculated decision to become a lawyer when she was only thirteen. Fourteen years, three hundred thousand dollars in tuition, and two progressively thicker lenses later, she'd been offered a junior position with a small firm in her Napa hometown—either *because* her last name was St. Pierre, or in spite of it. And today, at the weekly meeting, she was finally being assigned her own case.

At precisely eight-thirty-five, one porcelain cup of chamomile tea, one bowl of Greek yogurt, and half a banana later, she slid into her black Mercedes to make it to her law office in time for the crucial nine o'clock meeting.

She looked both ways before steering the sleek sedan out of the long gravel drive of Domaine St. Pierre onto Dry Creek Road. Her car cut a perpendicular path between rows of yellow-green mustard flower buds alternating with what appeared to be dead sticks wedged upright in the soil. It was only March, though. The sap was rising. By summer, the mustard would be over and those "sticks," laden with leaves and berries, would steal the show, drawing thousands upon thousands of tourists to Napa Valley—doubling her drive time to and from work. But this morning, there was no other vehicle in sight.

She double-checked her reflection in the rearview to make sure the gold clasp on her pearls lay on her collarbone, just so. Then she pinched an earlobe to secure a diamond ear stud, brushed a microscopic speck of lint from her shoulder and cupped the chignon at the base of her neck.

Satisfied that all was in order, she began a mental preview of the day. She fast-forwarded, picturing herself seated side by side with the firm's partners around the long conference table, eager for the chance to finally prove herself worthy of someday becoming the first female partner at Witmer, Robinson and Scott.

"Diana! Susanna! *¡Vuelve!* Come back!"

Esteban leaned on the handle of his pitchfork, grinning as he watched his mother toddle after a clutch of her errant Ameracaunas. Expertly, she snatched up a hen into the crook of her arm and brandished a threatening finger in her face. *"¡Chica traviesa!* You naughty girl. How many times do I have to tell you do not go down the lane, eh?" Beneath her long strokes, the chicken's feathers flickered iridescent gold, green, and orange in the morning light. She softened her tone to a tender purr. "My beautiful little *chica*."

Esteban shook his head. Madre was as fond of those stupid birds as she was of him and his sister. If possible, her attachment to her "girls" seemed to have only deepened, now that Esmerelda was married and living in Santa Rosa.

"Esteban! Can you look at the fence again? My *chicas* must have poked another hole somewhere," his mother pleaded, gently setting Marlena down with the others to shoo them back toward the paddock.

"Sí, Madre," he said, lapsing briefly into his native tongue.

Away from the farm, Esteban prided himself on his command of English. Mr. Bloomquist at Vintage High had even offered to write him a college recommendation.

"Your chem teacher said she'd write one, too," he'd coaxed. "We agree it would be a waste of your verbal and analytical skills not to continue your education. You could start out at NVCC and transfer to a four-year school later. . . ."

Esteban had been helping out on the family farm ever since he could lift a spade, but he'd never questioned why it was that plants were green. When he'd learned that what made them that way was a substance called chlorophyll that captured the sun's energy to make sugar out of air and water, he'd been fascinated. From then on, he'd been somewhat of a science geek.

After Mr. Bloomquist's offer, he'd imagined himself for a minute in a white lab coat, peering through a microscope at chloroplasts and ribosomes. The thought had made his scalp tingle.

But Esteban Morales was born to be a farmer. What would Padre do without him?

"This afternoon," he responded to Madre. First he needed to check on the effect of last night's rain on his tender lavender plants. The worst thing for lavender was mold.

Another stray—Natalia?—ran helter-skelter into Esteban's field of vision, down the muddy lane from where Padre had already thinned celery seedlings in the truck gardens earlier in the morning, past the paddock and the house toward Dry Creek Road. *¡Mierda!* Was he actually beginning to distinguish one of the flighty creatures from another?

"No this afternoon—now!" Madre scolded. She grabbed her broom from the porch and used it to sweep Natalia back toward the paddock. "You see this?" She gestured animatedly. "Before they all run onto the road and get hit by a car, and I have no chickens, no eggs, no money to pay the bills!"

Esteban chuckled under his breath. The Morales family would never be rich, yet they were hardly in dire straits. Losing a random eight-dollar chicken here and there wouldn't break the bank.

"Okay, okay."

Madre's appreciative grin was a reminder of her unconditional love, no matter how stern she pretended to be.

He continued in the direction of the shed. "I'll go get my tools."

Seconds later, he cringed to the squeal of rubber on asphalt and a sickening, avian screech.

Savvy slammed on the brakes the moment the chicken darted into view, but too late. She felt a thump, heard a squawk, and cringed. *I can't be late for work! Not today!* Yet something about the stricken expression on the face of the farm woman toddling toward her stabbed at her heart.

Mrs. Morales. She'd seen her stout silhouette a hundred times from a distance as she drove past the modest ranch house on Dry Creek Road, but she'd never met her next-door neighbor face-to-face. Still, thanks to Jeanne, the St. Pierre cook, she knew all about the Moraleses. Jeanne bought vegetables from their stand at the Napa farmers' market. As far back as grade school, Jeanne had been rattling on about the Moraleses, their daughter, Esmerelda, and son, what's-his-name. But while Jeanne had only good things to say about the family, Papa always said Mr. Morales was nothing but a big pain in the *derriere*.

Savvy threw the gearshift into park, got out, and strode around to the right front tire, bracing for what she might find.

Directly behind the front passenger-side tire lay the deceased—intact, thankfully, but motionless, its beak frozen open in its final squawk.

"Marlena!" The older woman stopped short at the edge of the lane. Her chest heaved with effort. Calloused palms flung in helplessness toward the dead animal. "*Marlena!*" she sobbed.

Savvy looked from Mrs. Morales's furrowed brow to the chicken—er, Marlena —and back.

Lips pressed into a tight line, she swallowed her squeamishness, squatting down for a better look. The last time she'd been this close to a chicken it had been covered in a delicate morel sauce.

What was she supposed to do? She glanced back up at Mrs. Morales to see her cross herself, then back down at Marlena. *Don't birds carry all kinds of diseases? Bird flu? Salmonella? Mites?*

She took a resigned breath, the farm odors of wet earth mingled with manure assaulting her senses, and steeled herself. This was all her fault. It was her responsibility to fix it.

Gingerly, she slid her bare hands under the hen's body. The unfamiliar feel of stiff feathers atop warm jelly—apparently Marlena had been neither smart nor athletic—brought up the taste of bile. Somehow she found the strength to swallow it back.

Slowly, she turned and gently deposited the animal into its owner's outstretched arms.

"*Dios mío.*" Mrs. Morales hugged the hen to a bosom that threatened to ooze from between the buttons of her shirt and rocked the bird, all the while chanting something that sounded like, *sana, sana, colita de rana*—whatever that meant. Obviously, the chicken had been a well-loved pet.

"I'm so sorry!" Savvy cried, torn between the urge to embrace the grieving woman and the longing for a hazmat shower.

And then from out of nowhere, an agrilicious, king-sized man in faded jeans, snug plaid shirt, and silver belt buckle the size of a turkey platter jogged up to them, and in a flash, Savvy forgot all about death and God and germs. She even forgot about work.

Chapter 2

Esteban stood with his back against the counter, arms folded in suspicion of the beautiful *fresa* sitting on the other side of the table.

Madre should be furious! So why had she insisted that he pull the woman's Mercedes into the lane for her, as if she were too distraught to do it herself? What girl that age drove a car like that, anyway? And how was it that, in the time it'd taken him to round up the rest of the chickens, set a two-by-four against the hole in the fence, and come into the house, that ritzy stranger now sat in his very own chair, pinky finger posed like the Queen of England's, sipping Madre's hastily brewed chamomile tea?

"My favorite," she purred to Madre, delicate nostrils quivering.

"Good for your nerves." His mother reached across the table to pat her hand consolingly.

She'd just killed one of Madre's prized Ameraucanas, and Madre was treating her as the victim instead of the perpetrator!

She was one of the prize offshoots of Xavier St. Pierre, the notorious grower, vintner, and landowner next door. Though he could see their house from his, he'd never gotten a close-up. Still, he'd been hearing stories about Chardonnay, Sauvignon, and Merlot all his life. Who in the valley hadn't?

Madre had been good friends with Jeanne, the St. Pierre cook, for years. Jeanne had reportedly been inconsolable when the girls had been sent to schools "back east"—a term that brought to mind thoroughbreds and country clubs—after Xavier's wife left him and died in a car crash in South America. When the girls—now young women—had returned from their respective schools last year, Jeanne had been ecstatic—even more so because the timing had coincided with Jeanne's own daughter's move to Portland.

Padre brooded every time Xavier St. Pierre's name came up. He said just because St. Pierre had come from an ancient line of grape growers, he thought he knew better than anyone else about *terreno*. About farming. Besides, this was America! Everyone started out equal. Or was supposed to.

Without warning, the woman raised lashes long and curly as a tendril on a pea vine. Or maybe they were only magnified by her thick glasses. Even through their lenses, Esteban recognized the intelligent curiosity in her brown eyes. When her lips curled into a polite smile, his heart stopped. Was it her skin, translucent as the petals of an apple blossom? The educated way she talked? Or her rosy scent, sweeter than the honey she stirred into her tea?

Don't forget what she did. That was *his* old wooden chair Madre had given her to sit in, her skinny butt only filling up half of it. He was struck by a pang of resentment, followed immediately by embarrassment when he eyed the chair from her perspective. He'd eaten how many meals from that chair—and only now noticed how badly its white paint was chipped, and that one of the rungs needed reglued. He glanced down at his muddy boots, comparing them to her fine leather shoes. He made his living in the fields. There was no shame in that. Defiantly, he lifted his chin. What was she to him, but a privileged, pampered wine princess whom he'd never get this close to again? She wouldn't be here now if she hadn't destroyed one of Madre's award-winning flock.

Like two old biddies, the women clucked away, their tones morphing from traumatized to apologetic to gossipy, all in the space of fifteen minutes.

Had Madre no pride? No family loyalty?

"I see Jeanne every Saturday morning. She's my most faithful customer. I can tell you what she buys each season." Madre began listing vegetables on knobby fingers. They were fairly clean now, but by August she wouldn't be able to get the green off them no matter how long she scrubbed. "Asparagus and peas in the early summer. After that, *pepinos*—how you say it?" She frowned, glancing at Esteban. You'd think she'd know by now. But Madre was used to relying on his help.

Esteban's eyes were busy combing over the human sunflower's shiny-sleek hair and her lithe body in an effort to memorize the creature that fate had unexpectedly brought. Despite his determination to hate her—scion of his father's worst enemy—her every movement captivated him.

"Esteban?" repeated his mother.

"Cucumbers," said Esteban, his sole contribution to the conversation since he'd walked in.

She held up a triumphant finger. "Cucumbers! And basil, and mint. Then peaches, peppers, and melons. Arugula and kale, into the fall. And always, my eggs . . ." Back to the chickens.

All at once, the eyes and mouth of the out-of-place kitchen goddess flew open wide.

"Omigod. My meeting!" She glanced at her gold watch. "I'm late!"

Halfway to the door, she caught herself. "Mrs. Morales, I want to give you some money to replace Marlena, but my purse is in the car, and I'm already super late for a very important meeting. . . ."

Madre shook her head. "No, Señorita Sauvignon. I will not hear of it. It was a accident. You don't owe me nothing. I will have Esteban fix the fence better this time."

Oh, so now it was his fault?

"Are you sure?" But the toe of one mud-spattered lambskin shoe was already over the threshold.

Esteban stood at the door watching her jog to her car, certain she'd never pass this way again.

Madre wouldn't let him forget about her, though. She'd be yakking about this for weeks. His resentment came roaring back and he felt his eyes narrow as Sauvignon St. Pierre disappeared into her car. If his shit-kickers had got her precious Mercedes floor mats dirty—well, too damn bad. He doubted she cleaned it herself, anyway. Probably had "people" for that.

Chapter 3

Savvy tore from the parking lot and breezed into the lobby of Witmer, Robinson and Scott, tucking a wayward strand of hair back into place. Outside the conference room, she took a belly breath and straightened her shoulders before making her entrance.

Robert Witmer looked up from his iPad. "Sauvignon. Nice of you to join us."

"Sorry. Little incident on the way to work."

All three partners looked up in unison. "Accident?" they sang in a chorus of hope.

"Nothing to worry about," she said with aplomb, sliding into a chair. She laid her forearms on the table, blew a wisp of hair out of her eye, and folded her hands. "No one was hurt."

"You don't need representation?" asked John Robinson, barely containing his disappointment.

"No, no. Not even worth discussing. I did have to stop, of course. But it's all taken care of."

"I always say, better safe than sorry. Might not be a bad idea to go to the hospital, get yourself checked out."

Savvy waved away his suggestion. "No. No need."

Robert cleared his throat. "We were just finishing up. I moved this item to the end of the agenda. Group calling themselves Napa Terroir Investments—NTI—is looking to acquire a piece of property in the Oak Knoll District between Yountville and Napa. It's not big. Talking price per acre, though, it's one of the most valuable pieces of real estate in the valley."

"I know that area. That's a sweet spot between the warm Up-valley and the southern end," said John.

"Warm enough for cab, cool enough for chardonnay," added Mike.

Just like everyone else in the valley, he thought he was an expert in all things wine.

"If you say so. It *is* one of the few parcels of Oak Knoll ground that isn't planted in grapes yet," continued Robert. "Savvy, this seems like the perfect case for you to get your feet wet. Show us what you're made of."

"Is it on the market?" Savvy asked.

"No."

"Wouldn't they do better to consult a Realtor?"

"As you know, your law license empowers you to act as a real estate broker. Besides, one of the partners is an old friend of mine. We'll work it so that you get a nice commission."

"Yes, sir." She wasn't an expert in real estate law. Wasn't an expert in *any* kind of law—*yet*. That's what apprenticeships were for. She had to start somewhere, didn't she?

"Anyone have anything else?" asked Robert.

"Hold it," said Mike Scott, pointing to Savvy's wrist. "Is that blood?"

All three men leaned in, narrowing their eyes. Savvy bent her elbow to examine her cuff.

"That?" She winced inwardly at the nickel-sized brown dot and snatched a tissue from the box in the middle of the table. "Not blood. There was no blood. Just a little . . . dirt, that's all."

Slowly, the men sat back again, regret filling their faces.

"Then we're adjourned, gentlemen—and Savvy," said Robert.

She made a beeline for the restroom, where she sniffed her wrist. Smelled like iron. Chicken blood! *Gross*. Surprising she hadn't noticed it earlier. She was blessed—or cursed, depending on circumstances—with a sense of smell so acute it was sometimes overwhelming. Hastily, she maneuvered her forearm directly under the wall dispenser and pumped a gob of antibacterial soap straight onto the stain.

Just when the lather was at its foamy peak, the lavatory door swung open and in walked Mr. Witmer's assistant, Helen.

All the firm's assistants were shared equally by the professionals, except Helen. She never passed up the opportunity to tell people that she'd been with Mr. Witmer since he'd opened the law office back in the Stone Age, and it appeared as though she hadn't changed her hairstyle since. Helen took one look at the pile of suds on Savvy's arm and raised a judgmental brow.

Savvy smiled. "Coffee," she said. "Clumsy me. Now my sleeve'll be damp all day."

"Best be more careful." Helen went into a stall and closed the door.

Savvy's face fell. It'd been months since she'd started at the firm, and the assistants were still giving her the cold shoulder, despite her wooing them with donuts, wine, and anything else she could think of.

Oh well. She had more pressing things on her mind this morning.

Poor Marlena, she thought as she scrubbed. *Poor Mrs. Morales.* Aside from them, what about her son, the god of agriculture, sleeping within half a mile of her very own bed each night? How was it that they had never crossed paths before?

Esteban. Silently, Savvy practiced wrapping her tongue around the name while she held her wrist under the faucet and waited for the suds to subside. From the moment he'd appeared on the scene of the accident, her nerves had sprung to red alert. He'd brought with him a clean, springtime scent, all rain and new grass. She'd had a rogue wish that time would stop and everyone would freeze in place so she could circle him the way she'd once circled Michelangelo's sculpture of David at the Academia in Florence, scrutinizing every inch. But time hadn't stopped. Instead, he'd tormented her, staring at her with his arms folded and that expression of disdain, the whole time she was drinking her tea.

When the water ran clear, she blotted her sleeve with paper towels, patting it dry the best she could. This morning was probably the closest she would ever get to Esteban. What did an ambitious attorney have in common with a farm boy who still lived under his parents' roof, anyway?

Complicating matters further, Papa had this thing against Mr. Morales. Exiting the restroom, she sighed. Esteban would join the David in her mind. Larger than life. Cold as marble. And totally out of reach.

Back at her desk, she opened the folder her boss had given her. Inside the cover was a memo signed by Don Smith, general partner of Napa Terroir Investments, authorizing her to make an initial offer of 1.5 million dollars for a certain five-acre parcel of land. Behind that was a local tax map of the property outlining its current assessed value, zoning, and other pertinent data. The lot was a small rectangle with frontage on Dry Creek Road, surrounded on three sides by much larger tracts of ground.

Wait a minute. Savvy's breath caught. She knew those ridges to the tract's north. She and her sisters had spent their early years roaming them at will, while their pretty French au pairs, who had been in America mainly to meet boys, flirted with the pickers.

Who was willing to pay such an exorbitant price for the paltry slice of land wedged in between those big tracts?

Anyone and everyone who wants to grow grapes, that's who. California wines were in high demand, even by European drinkers. The Napa Valley was finite. Only about forty thousand acres, compared to a hundred eighty-five in the Loire Valley, for example. They weren't making any more of it.

The offer was fair: land on the valley floor was going for three hundred thousand an acre, according to recent comparable sales. And virtually everyone agreed—the highest and best use of that land was viniculture.

Everyone, that was, except the Moraleses. They were still doing what they'd always done, eking out a living raising vegetables and chickens.

As she flipped through the remaining documents, she smiled. *Looks like I'll be seeing Esteban again, after all.* Her smile grew until she felt it all the way up to her eyes. Thanks to her new assignment, she could more than atone for making a fricassee of Marlena. In fact, she had news that might make Esteban and his family very, very happy.

Within the hour, she was knocking on the Moraleses' door with giddy anticipation. This time, she brought good tidings instead of bad. The cellophane surrounding a Cymbidium orchid, her peace offering, crackled in her grip. She'd also picked up a sympathy card and a prepaid debit card for triple the estimated cost of your average oven-stuffer.

Chapter 4

Esteban's lavender plants didn't look so good. He propped his hands on his hips, glaring down at where the experimental seedlings struggled to hold up their heads in the soupy soil. The valley floor was still saturated from a series of early spring rainstorms ferried inland by the Pineapple Express. Winegrapes didn't care—they went dormant in the winter—but lavender was a whole other animal.

That wasn't the only thing eating him. Ball-busting as farm chores might be, they left his mind free to wander. All day long, he hadn't been able to get Sauvignon St. Pierre out of his head.

While patching the hole in the chicken wire, he relived the entire incident down on Dry Creek Road.

Shoveling compost onto the strawberry patch, he thought of her delicately crossed ankles as she sat his rustic kitchen chair. He'd never be able to sit on that chair again without that image coming to mind.

Then, this afternoon, setting cabbages with Padre had brought back the memory of her chocolate-brown eyes. Those dark-framed glasses she sported were a crime against nature. He imagined peeling them off her face, followed by the pins that held back her hair. . . . *Why not go whole hog? I still have two dozen cabbages to set out.* Slowly unzipping her dress . . .

The sound of a car coming up the lane interrupted his fantasy.

The black Mercedes! She was back!

Padre heard it too. Esteban had filled him in on the events of the morning when he'd returned from breakfast with his *amigos*. At Esteban's mention of the killer's name, his father's eyes had grown leery. But his concern had quickly faded. Say what you will about the girls next door being spoiled heiresses, they all had jobs. The sight of their matching Mercedes on their way to work was a daily occurrence. Madre had got the lowdown firsthand, from Jeanne. Sauvignon was a lawyer, Chardonnay ran some kind of kids' charity, and Merlot made jewelry. (*¡Mierda!* To have to go through life with those names! There wasn't enough money in the world to make up for that.)

Like Padre always said, accidents happened all the time on farms. Besides, the chickens were Madre's business. Padre was in charge of the truck gardens. All in all, he didn't seem too concerned.

The nearer the Mercedes got, the harder Esteban's heart thudded. Through the budding branches of a magnolia tree, he watched as her car stopped directly in front of the house. A shapely leg emerged from the driver's seat. Flowers. *Sí.* That explained it.

"An 'I'm sorry' present for Madre," he said to his father. Padre grunted and went back to work. Esteban followed suit, so Padre wouldn't notice his pulse pounding as if he'd just come up from an extended free dive off the coast of Salt Point.

All Esteban could do was steal an occasional glimpse house-ward while his imagination ran unchecked over what was going on inside those four walls. Señorita Sauvignon had been in there way too long merely to hand over some flowers. Madre had probably offered her some more tea, and was now talking her ear off again.

"Esteban!" He jumped when he heard Madre call.

Padre's back slowly straightened from over his hoe, but Esteban didn't dare meet his eyes, to give away the eagerness he felt emblazoned all over his face.

"Come here!"

As he made his way to the house, Esteban glanced at his filthy hands and his dirt-spattered jeans. He resisted the impulse to run a hand through his matted shock of hair when he realized that would only make it worse. *Mierda.* He wished now that that girl had never returned. Everything about her, from her fine-boned figure to her fancy East Coast accent, made him feel coarse and uncivilized. Come to think of it, he could never risk bedding her. His heavy body would crush her like a grape.

Madre met him at the open door, eyes filled with concern. "Señorita Sauvignon brought some papers. I told her you would look at them."

Cozy as ever in his chair, Sauvignon smiled up at him. He nodded a terse greeting and went over to the big farmhouse sink to scrub the soil off his hands the best he could before accepting her handshake. Her pale skin felt smooth and soft as a baby's in his rough brown one, but her grip was that of a confident businesswoman.

"Tell my son what you told me," his mother ordered.

Today had started out like any other day until *she* had come along, turning everything upside down. On her first visit, Sauvignon had been focused entirely on Madre. She'd all but ignored Esteban, making it easy for him to stand back and observe. Now her attention was zeroed in on him. The electricity flowing from her body through his made it damn near impossible to follow the message she delivered.

She sat erect as a garden stake, elbows anchored on the table, creamed and polished hands fluttering like butterflies to make her points.

The sight of her moving lips mesmerized him. The sound of her voice obscured the meaning of her words. He eyed the closed folder before her, wishing she would have mercy on him and just shut up, be still, and let him read whatever was in it for himself.

To make matters worse, Madre's anxious eyes were glued to his face, as he filled his role as family representative.

"Do you understand?" Sauvignon peered directly at him through her glasses.

His silence must make him seem like a total bonehead. Somehow, he'd managed to ferret out the key facts. "There's been a mistake. Our place isn't for sale."

She wasn't fazed a bit. "I understand. You aren't actively seeking a buyer. Be that as it may, an offer has been made. A very attractive one. Let me show you what other, comparable properties have gone for in the past year." Scooting her chair closer to his, she opened the folder and pulled out some papers. He leaned in to read the fine print, following along as she pointed out the other transactions. She smelled like roses. When she finished, she and Madre looked at him and waited.

He sat back and studied her. She wasn't short by any means, but at his six-foot-five, he could eat soup off her head. He folded his arms across his chest. "This farm is my father's lifeblood. He would never sell it."

The ball was back in Sauvignon's court. Madre's head turned to her. "Do you think I could talk to him?"

Madre waited expectantly for Esteban's response.

"He doesn't speak English."

"Esteban speaks for him," interjected Madre.

"I see."

He watched her mull that over.

"What if I had the documents translated?"

Esteban's breath stopped. There was an awkward pause as he waited to hear if Madre would confess to Padre's number-one short-coming.

The pause lengthened, until Madre finally admitted, "Geraldo doesn't read."

There it was, the humiliating truth. There was nothing he could do about it.

Sauvignon thought about that for a few seconds, then switched gears. "Mrs. Morales, according to these records, you've lived here for quite a while."

Madre nodded. "A long time. Geraldo's *tío* Esteban—" She halted, looking at her son for help.

"Uncle," translated Esteban.

Madre nodded. "Geraldo's uncle Esteban had a Christmas tree farm here. He was a smart man. Like a second father to Geraldo." She smiled fondly at the memory. "That's why we named our son for him. We moved in with him here when little Esteban was six years old. Left our parents, brothers, sisters, and all our friends, to give our son a better life in America. When *Tío* died, he gave us the house."

"If you don't mind my asking, do you own the property free and clear?"

She wanted to know if it was mortgaged, Esteban knew.

"*Sí,* yes," Madre replied, lighting up as if she'd heard that term before. "Free and clear."

Sauvignon leaned into Madre, staring at her unblinking through her thick lenses. "Mrs. Morales, do you understand how much money a million and a half dollars is? You could buy a beautiful new home, almost anywhere you please. Have the lifestyle you've always dreamed of."

Madre shrugged. "But I already have my house. We like it here."

Savvy sat back and thought some more. "What are your plans for the future?"

His parents were in their late fifties yet looked older, thanks to a lifetime working outside in all kinds of weather.

Madre raised her eyebrows. "We'll just grow old, right here." She tapped her thick fingers lightly on the table where her work-worn hand rested.

Hard as they hung on to the old ways, his parents lived squarely in the present. They didn't dwell in the past or fret too much about the future.

Madre smiled politely, while Esteban's satisfied expression said, *See? You're screwed. Now, get out of my chair and go back to your big white mansion and leave us alone.*

Sauvignon looked calmly from mother to son, but he sensed her brainstorming behind those ugly glasses. She arose from her—*his*—chair and crossed the floor to the window above the sink full of freshly washed spinach. His eyes became lasers, burning every detail of her lanky body into his memory. She wasn't perfect. Could use a few pounds, for his taste. With a graceful hand, she eased back the ruffled curtain to peer out into the garden where Padre toiled.

"You must be very proud of Mr. Morales. He's a hard worker, isn't he?"

Madre nodded vigorously. "*Sí.* Nobody works harder than Geraldo."

"A good provider."

"Oh, *sí.* His family always comes first. He gives us a good living."

"He must get very tired."

"Yes. Just last night, his muscles ache so much, I rub his back for half an hour. And his blood pressure . . ."

Savvy let the curtain drop. "Would you talk to your husband"— she glanced to Esteban—"your father, for me? Maybe he's had other thoughts since the last time this subject came up. You wouldn't want him to miss out on an opportunity that he might actually welcome, would you?"

Pretty *and* smart. That only made him trust her less.

"I'll talk to him," said Esteban. "But now I have to get back to work. We have . . . " *Cabbages to plant?* It sounded so . . . menial.

For a fleeting second, Sauvignon looked affronted at being dismissed, but she recovered quickly. "Of course." She returned to the table to gather her belongings. The click of high heels on the linoleum, the rosy scent, her striking appearance . . . it all added up to more femininity than that little room had ever witnessed. Handing him the business card she pulled from her bag, she said, "You'll call me?"

"*Sí.*" *Mierda,* she unhinged him. "I mean, yes."

"One minute!" Madre leapt up and went over to the counter where she'd been cleaning produce before the second interruption of this memorable day. She stuffed a bunch of early radishes into a paper bag and thrust it toward Sauvignon. "Take these. For Jeanne. She adores them with her baguette and butter in the morning."

"I'll see that she gets them."

"Esteban will walk you to your car."

Just what he wanted—the chance to feel like a second-class citizen a little longer. He had been raised to be respectful though. He leapt to his feet to get to the door before their guest did.

"Thanks," she said with mild surprise.

Was it so shocking that a ruffian like him knew the most basic etiquette?

Without Madre's presence to smooth things over, the trek to her car was awkward. Esteban observed her every nuance . . . how she dodged the rocks in the lane in those heels, the way she hugged her big leather shoulder bag to her side, like a shield. He may only have a high school education, but he had the instincts of a Skyline Park mountain lion. Behind the sophisticated armor, something about her gave him the sense that she was as rattled as he. He closed the distance between them. Now he could gaze down onto the tender skin of her nape, where a few fine hairs had come loose from the knot at the base of her skull. As if feeling his eyes on her neck, she tucked in a wisp with cherry-red fingertips.

When they got to the Mercedes, he squeezed the chrome handle and swept open the door, noting how the small of her back curved beneath her simple dress when she got in . . . the stretch of calf between her hemline and ankle. He closed her in with a solid *kachunk.*

Then he folded his arms and watched her face reflected in the side mirror as she drove down the lane, intent on the road before her. When he finally lost sight of her, he turned to go back to work.

Somehow, though, everything seemed different. Empty. As if Sauvignon St. Pierre had sucked the life force out of the farm and taken it with her.

Mierda.

Not only that—she'd left him harder than his spade handle.

"What did the daughter of the devil want this time?" Standing over him where he firmed the dirt around a seedling, Padre pulled a rumpled bandana from his back pocket. It had taken him a whole hour to bring up Sauvignon's second visit. Esteban had used the time to set the rest of the cabbage plants, trying to get over the double whammy of seeing her twice in the same day and considering the pros and cons of her offer.

"She was here on business," he replied in Spanish. He stood, tamping the dirt with the toe of his boot for good measure. "Someone put in an offer our land."

"Someone?" Padre snorted. "You mean *el diablo Francés*. How much did that old *cabrón* offer this time?"

Esteban frowned, confused. "What do you mean, 'this time'?"

"This isn't the first time Xavier St. Pierre has tried to get his hands on my property."

Esteban pulled Sauvignon's crumpled card from his front pocket. He reread the name of her firm, then extended the card toward Padre before jerking it back at the last second, mindful of offending him. "Not her father this time. An investment group. The name's on the papers back at the house. She only works for the law firm that's representing them."

"Two visits in one day? You expect me to believe this is a coincidence? I'm not stupid. Trust me. St. Pierre has a plan."

"How do you hatch a plot to run over a stray chicken?"

"Don't put anything past Xavier St. Pierre."

Esteban kept his expression neutral. Padre's wrath wasn't confined to St. Pierre. He resented all the big-name vintners, who he claimed were "taking over" the valley, now that wine was such a huge commodity. That's all he and his group of longtime expats talked about at their breakfasts down at the diner.

Modest as their little farm was by some standards, Padre had found success beyond the wildest dreams of the young, uneducated *hombre Michoacán* who'd immigrated to California two decades ago, but it wasn't in his nature to boast. Besides, bragging about your good fortune was taboo, according to Padre. It attracted something he called *envidia*.

"Goes without saying we aren't going to sell. Still, it might be a good idea to read over the offer anyway, see what people are thinking about our land."

Padre grunted.

"I'll read the papers to you after supper," said Esteban.

Chapter 5

During dinner, Savvy shared the events of her day with the family, starting with the death of Marlena and ending with the offer she'd made on behalf of NTI.

"The Moraleses should keep a better watch on their assets," declared Papa. "What if you had been injured, running over that free-ranging bird?"

Savvy made a face. "It was an accident. A hole in the fence. And don't call Marlena an asset. She was Mrs. Morales's pet. You act like it's a barrio over there, like they have mongrels wagging all over the place and a goat on a spit in the yard. It's actually a very tidy little farm." She took a bite of risotto. "You'd be impressed, if you ever took the time to be neighborly, go over and introduce yourself."

"Farmette," Papa corrected her. "Morales is an imbecile. Winegrapes would bring in more than ten times the price per ton than his peas and tomatoes. The valley floor is rich in calcium." He kissed his bunched fingertips. "Perfect for pinot."

How many times had she heard that? "Anyway, this is my first case, and I have to admit, I'm kind of excited about it," she said.

"We are so proud of you," said Char, the middle child. The peacekeeper.

"So, are they willing to sell?" asked Meri, the youngest sister.

"Too soon to tell. One-point-five million is only the initial offer. NTI is willing to go higher. Mr. Morales doesn't speak English, so his son, Esteban, is acting as a go-between."

Papa looked up from cutting his filet. "You realize that if you are successful with this case, *ma chère,* that will be your first step toward making partner."

She knew. Since the day she'd been hired, she'd spent every

minute laying the groundwork. Working overtime, offering to take on extra responsibilities—everything she could think of to ingratiate herself to the partners in Witmer, Robinson and Scott.

Making partner meant more to her than mere paternal approval. Somebody had to hold this family together. Take care of her sisters, keep an eye on Papa. Half the time, he was all about business. The other half, he was carousing with starlets half his age or getting into some other kind of trouble. Savvy never stopped worrying what his next shenanigan would be. Because it would always be something.

After supper, Savvy and her sisters did the dishes.

"Have you thought about a good time for us to discuss your prenup, now that you're engaged?" Savvy asked Char, handing her a dripping plate to dry.

Char gave a bored sigh. "Not really."

"Don't put it off. I can't tell you how important it is. If things go sour, you don't want to leave things up to the courts. There are any number of reasons why—"

"I know, I know," said Char, rolling her eyes. She sang the litany of reasons Savvy had drilled into her like a song. "To learn more about each other, marriage is a business relationship, future alimony, property settlement, yada yada yada."

"Go ahead and make fun," said Savvy. "Someday you'll thank me." She turned to Meri. "And that goes for you, too."

Meri held up her left hand. "Do you see a ring on this finger?"

"He gave you the gold ingot and the rock. Is it my fault you haven't made it yet? You spend half your nights with him in the city! You have to start thinking about these things." When she turned back to the sink, she felt her sisters' eyes connecting behind her back.

"Cocoa Puffs," one of them whispered dramatically, loud enough for Savvy to hear.

They could mock her all they wanted. Savvy considered it her responsibility to see that they were taken care of. Wasn't that why she'd become a lawyer in the first place?

Savvy concluded her elaborate bedtime routine—makeup remover, cleanser, toner, and moisturizer. She'd intended to take work to bed, but she was too keyed up. She wandered downstairs into the kitchen, where Jeanne was seated at the table, planning the next week's meals. During all those years in exile back east, the kitchen—

the beating heart of every home—was the room Savvy had missed the most. Jeanne ran this one like a well-oiled machine. The counters had been wiped, fresh tea towels had been laid out for the next day, and the dishwasher hummed in the background.

Though she wasn't hungry, she opened the fridge and peered inside.

"French women do not snack," said Jeanne.

Savvy sighed and came out empty-handed. "I know."

"Where are the others?"

"Out with their paramours," replied Jeanne.

This past year had been golden for Meri and Char. Each had stumbled upon her soul mate.

"And you? Why don't you go out more often?"

"I have a brief to read."

"You work too hard for such a young lady. How are you going to meet anyone?"

"I'm not looking for anyone." Savvy poured herself a glass of spring water and walked to the window.

"Well, if you were, it would be too dark to see anything out there. Come. Tell me what's wrong."

"Nothing's wrong. It's just—I'm waiting for a call."

Jeanne lifted a shaped brow. Ever since Savvy had graduated from law school and moved back to the winery, Jeanne and her sisters were always on the lookout for Savvy to meet someone. "Someone special?"

Savvy's head whipped around.

"Ah. So there *is* someone."

Savvy bit her tongue while Jeanne casually licked a finger and flipped a page in her cooking magazine.

"Not really. Just business."

"Must be very *important* business."

Savvy went over and slid into the seat next to her. Char and Meri came to Savvy for advice. But Savvy had no one older and wiser to confide in except Jeanne.

"It's Esteban." She'd already told Jeanne about the dead chicken incident before dinner, while helping her stir the risotto.

"You're waiting to hear if his papa will agree to sell their property."

Savvy smiled glumly while Jeanne studied an ad for soy milk as if it were the most interesting concept since the Swedish AGA range she'd insisted Papa install for her, twenty years back.

"I should've given him a deadline to get back to me, but I didn't think of it. Now I have no idea when I'll hear from him."

"It has been but a few hours, no?"

"Yessss..." She sounded to herself like a pathetic, lovelorn teenager instead of an officer of the court.

"Next time, you'll know to give a time limit. I would say you could call him, but this is never a good idea for a woman to call a man."

Savvy huffed. "It's not like that! Like I said, this is business. Only business." She adored Jeanne, even if her advice was sometimes old school.

"Of course," said Jeanne, pursing her lips. She took off her reading glasses and set them on the table. "And you have no personal interest whatsoever in Esteban Morales. Is that what you wish me to believe?"

Savvy's heart rate speeded up. "No—I mean yes! I mean—" Her sheepish grin was a dead giveaway.

"Of course you don't. Why would you be interested in a kind, hardworking man from an honorable family? Perhaps you don't like his strong arms, his capable hands, his soulful eyes...."

"Jeanne!" Savvy's face heated. Jeanne was like a mother to her. Mothers didn't say things like that to their daughters. Did they?

Jeanne shrugged. "Then there is no reason for concern. Go to bed. It is only business, as you said. He will call when he will call."

Big help she turned out to be.

Savvy turned and padded out of the kitchen, up the sweeping staircase, and down the long hallway to her room. But her thoughts were too scattered to focus on her brief. She fell asleep hours later, dreaming that Esteban's face was on the body of the David at the Academia, and she and all the other visitors were circling him with admiration.

Chapter 6

One morning, a week after the real estate offer, Esteban waited in vain for his father to join him in the fields after breakfast. Gradually, he worked his way closer to the house so he could ask Madre where he'd gone.

"He went to the doctor. Nothing serious. To check his blood pressure."

He already knew the gist of what Padre would say. There were only so many ways to say no. But he couldn't put off Sauvignon much longer.

It was lunchtime when Padre finally pulled up the lane. At the table, while Madre related the latest news about Esmerelda's kids in detail—Lily had gotten an A on her first-grade science project, Jenny had fallen off her bike and brush-burned her knees—the men listened and chewed their sandwiches. When the meal was over, they returned to separate areas of the field.

Once the lettuce had been weeded, he took a break from the vegetable gardens to check on his lavender experiments. He was cutting a stem from a specimen of Lavendula Goodwin Creek Grey when his father ambled over. "So? Have you given any more thought to that offer?" he asked, sniffing the cutting's pungent scent.

"I have plenty of good food to eat, a comfortable home, and a fat wife."

"That's your answer?"

"Anything more than that only invites *envidia.*"

"Envy."

"Undeserved good fortune often ends with something bad happening."

"Like karma?" He tossed the sprig of Grey and went on to the next variety.

"I've seen it happen again and again in my life," warned Padre. "There is only one more thing I want before I die. What every man wants."

A grandson. Esteban had been hearing that all his adult life—more, since Esmerelda had birthed her third daughter. Even if his sister in Santa Rosa did someday produce a boy, the kid wasn't likely to return to Napa to farm. Esmerelda's husband was a teacher, so it was pretty much a no-brainer. Their kids would be the first in the Morales bloodline to go to college.

"You want your grandson to be legitimate?"

Padre crossed himself. "You have to ask me such a question?"

"That's not happening anytime soon. I don't even have a prospect."

"You go out enough. Open your eyes! There are *chulas* everywhere."

"None that I want to spend the rest of my life with."

"Maybe you should stop playing with flowers and find one. I'm not getting any younger."

"I'm only twenty-seven!"

"I married your mother when I was eighteen, and good thing I did. It took us another fourteen years until the Lord gave us a son."

Esteban knew the story by heart. In their quest to conceive a boy, his parents had visited dozens of doctors, even a few *curanderos*—folk healers—in the years after Esmerelda came along.

If Padre was so glad to be in America, why did he cling so hard to the old ways? Getting tied down with a wife and kid was the furthest thing from Esteban's mind. When he wasn't trying to find the best strain of lavender for the Morales farm's micro-climate, he was into hiking and diving with Tomas and George and the rest of his crew. And Padre didn't know how right he was: there *were* women everywhere. Esteban didn't do too bad with them, either. In fact, his record was pretty impressive, if he said so himself. No reason to limit himself to just one.

Deep down, he knew what was really bothering his father.

Where Padre came from, infertility was an embarrassment, a real threat to a man's *machismo*. Padre worried he might have passed down what he considered his inadequacies to his son. That Esteban was like lavandin—a mule. A hybrid. Unable to reproduce. He was anxious to be proved wrong.

But Esteban was getting sidetracked. He still had to tell Sauvignon *something*.

Bodega was hopping.

"Isn't this better than staying home, waiting for your phone to ring?" asked Meri, seated next to her.

It had been one long, agonizingly slow week, waiting for Esteban to call. Her whole career depended on Mr. Morales's decision.

"You can't work twenty-four-seven," Meri said. "No harm in one glass of wine at the end of the day."

"Look who's talking about not working," Char retorted. "The successful jeweler who's branching out into—"

Intent on advising Savvy, Meri interrupted Char's accolades. "Keep your eyes open. Who knows, you might even *meet* someone."

Savvy rolled her eyes.

"Stranger things have happened," Meri said.

Had it come to this? Was her baby sister really coaching her on how to pick up men now? She wasn't dumb. When—*if*—Savvy ever had time to spare for a man, she could find one herself.

Down the bar, a familiar cellar master from another winery waved and Savvy smiled back.

She had to admit, this spot was unique. Tourists considered the Italian restaurant a can't-miss wine country dining experience. At the same time, the locals knew it as a hangout for everyone from the lowliest picker to the most illustrious winemaker.

"If I ever become a barfly, this will be my bar of choice," said Meri. "It's a Stan-free zone. Here, I feel like I'm either *well*-known or *un*known."

"Stan-free?"

"Stalker-slash-fan."

Savvy jumped a foot when her phone vibrated. She grabbed it from where she'd placed it on the bar, within easy reach.

"Hello?"

"This is Esteban Morales."

The classy surroundings filled with satisfied murmurings faded away. All that existed was his voice. She clutched her phone closer to her ear.

"Hi! How are you?"

"Good. I have an answer for you."

After a week, now Esteban didn't mince words.

"Do you want to meet somewhere?" she asked.

"Where are you now?"

She blinked the restaurant back into focus. "Bodega."

"See you in ten."

Her pulse leapt. She found herself second-guessing her customary little black dress and worrying about whether her lipstick was smeared from the two sips of wine she'd drunk so far. Char and Meri were conversing with someone at the other end of the bar. She slid off her stool and went to the ladies' room to spray on a little more Miss Dior before he arrived.

Even with their backs to the door, it was a cinch picking out the St. Pierre heiresses, lined up like a row of Easter tulips at the bar: same size and shape, different colors, delicately sipping wine from balloon-shaped glasses. One chestnut-colored twisted knot, one sizzling blond, and a brunette with jelly-bean streaks. Hair color aside, all three were cut from the same mold. Lay a level along the head of the one in the middle and the arc would be perfectly centered.

What was it about them that had that cluster of men in slim-cut suits without socks jockeying for position? There was no obvious sign of wealth, no come-fuck-me clothes. Maybe it was their tall, slim bodies. That air of confidence without cockiness. Whatever it was, what everyone said was true: those three *were* God's gift to Napa. At least, on the outside. He still didn't trust Savvy's motives.

There were no seats left at the bar, yet one glance at Esteban cruising toward the French twist and the competition parted like a dust devil in a cornfield. Size mattered.

Behind Savvy's nerdy glasses, her eyes widened with appreciation at his clean jeans and fresh shirt. If he saw her a hundred times, he'd never get used to those specs. To cover up a face like that was just wrong. They were a barrier between him and those liquid brown eyes, that flawless skin. Those plump lips . . .

"Hell-o?" she trilled, arching a brow.

"Hey." If he was going to be hanging with a woman like her, he'd better up his conversational game.

The bartender asked what he was drinking. When he leaned in to be heard above the din, the heavenly scent of lily of the valley, warmed by her blood, assaulted his senses. He'd already come to associate the scent of roses with her, but this one wasn't bad, either.

"The usual. Draft."

"Well?" She couldn't wait another minute. "What did your father say?"

"It's like I told you. We have no interest in selling our land," he said, one hand on his beer—a welcome reward after a hard day in the fields—the other resting on the back of her bar stool.

"What *exactly* did he say?"

He tried and failed to drag his eyes off the sight of her rosy fingertip, tracing the rim of her wineglass. "You have to understand who he is. Who *we* are."

"So tell me." She swiveled her stool until her knees bumped against his hip. On his other side, the crowd hemmed him in.

He inhaled to get ready for his speech. "Everyone's a farmer, down in the Michoacán. My father grew up raising avocados, garbanzos, lemons, corn—you name it. There's nothing he can't grow." Except, maybe lavender. But it wasn't Padre who was messing around with that. Padre was too practical . . . or was sane the better word?

"Padre brought us here when land was still dirt cheap. For years, we helped his uncle work his farm, and in return he left the property to us. But even though Padre's a citizen now, the way he lives his life is still like it was in the Michoacán. The biggest difference is here, he can make a much better living."

Sauvignon listened intently. "What about you?"

He studied her face, looking for the meaning behind her words.

"What do you want to do with your life?" she repeated.

He swigged his beer. That kind of impractical, philosophical question was only pondered by people like her. He glanced over at the men with fifty-dollar haircuts hovering around her sisters. People of privilege.

"Farming is in my blood."

"That's not what I asked."

He laughed drily. "Kind of alien to me, that anyone can do whatever he wants with his life."

"Why is that?"

He thought for a minute. "It's not just what I want. There are other people to think about. Like my mother and father."

"I'm sure your parents want you to be happy."

She didn't get it. That farm was Padre's identity. Without it, he was nothing. He'd be wrecked if his only son gave up on it, after he'd devoted his life to nailing down a piece of the American dream for him. "Maybe what's best for my family *is* what will make me happiest."

"Say you didn't happen to like farming. What would happen then?"

"You don't do it because you like it," he explained. "You just do it. For the people you love. Who love you."

"So, it's about honor."

"You could call it that. I call it doing what's right for the people you care most about."

She shrugged. "Whatever. It's not like you *have* to do something other than farm."

But the reality was that Esteban couldn't imagine a life without his hands in the dirt. "I like growing things."

"So, you see yourself walking in your father's footsteps? Farming the same patch of land he did for the rest of your life?"

When she rotated back toward the bar to retrieve her wine, her knees brushed against his fly this time, prompting his eyes to move downward to her skirted thighs. He took a long pull on his beer and tried not think about what they looked like naked.

Concentrate. He *did* have a dream—even if Padre thought it was harebrained. What if he confided in her and then failed to achieve it? She would know. Even if he ran into her fifty years from now, *she would know.*

This conversation needed to be over. She was the enemy. Letting her in was too hard . . . in so many ways. He was only going to have one beer with her, say what needed to be said, and then be on his way. Even now, his friends were waiting for him at a bar in town. Her prodding questions brought his deepest desires uncomfortably close to the surface, kindling something powerful. Or maybe it was her knees rubbing against his *verga.*

"You really want to know?"

She lifted one slim shoulder. "You've got to have dreams. Otherwise, what's the point?" she asked, with all the self-assurance money could buy.

"Easy for you."

In a snap, her smile faded, eyes filled with resentment.

"Sorry. That wasn't fair."

"Seriously? No one just wakes up one day, and bang, they're a lawyer. You can't *buy* a passing grade on the bar exam."

"I said I was sorry." He was really fucking this up. She angled back toward the bar, robbing him of her attention . . . leaving him desperate to win her back. Which made no sense whatsoever.

"I have this idea to start a lavender farm," he blurted. As soon as the words left his mouth he felt stripped naked before God and the public. He looked around to see if anyone else had heard.

Sauvignon merely sipped at her drink and thought. Judging by the non-effect his revelation had on her, he might as well have asked her to pass the Sriracha. He tilted his empty glass, wishing there were still beer in it. His mouth felt like Death Valley.

Thankfully the bartender chose that moment to reappear. They had good help in this place.

"Another draft, Esteban?"

The fact that the bartender knew his name got her attention. He nodded yes to the beer, then, with another cocky impulse, turned to her and asked, "You hungry?"

She hesitated, weighing her options. "I guess I could eat a little something."

"What's today's *pesce crudo*, Raoul?"

"We have some abalone sashimi. First catch of the season. We're full tonight, but you can eat here, at the bar."

Abalone . . . what Esteban had been waiting for all winter. He gave Raoul a thumbs-up. "Give us a double order. And give Sauvignon another glass of"—he knew little about wine—"whatever she's drinking."

Chapter 7

"I eat here every week," Esteban said in answer to Savvy's blank expression.

With a graciousness that would put some of the most sophisticated men of her acquaintance to shame, he continued without pointing out how elitist she was to be surprised that he, a mere truck farmer, was also a regular at one of the valley's finest eateries. "It's hard to get fresh abs without driving over to the coast or down to the city. Unless I dive for them myself."

"You dive for abalone? I hear that's really dangerous." She owed him her polite consideration after her faux pas, yet her interest was real.

He tilted his head in acknowledgment. "They lose a couple of divers every year. Riptides. Exhaustion. Guys get stuck in a crevice and panic. It happens."

"You risk your life for a sea snail?"

Raoul slapped down a matched set of silverware rolled in white linen. Savvy smiled gratefully at the guy next to her who offered up his chair to Esteban so he didn't have to eat standing. A moment later, their abalone arrived on a bed of romaine, garnished with kelp, lemon slices, and a purple blossom.

"I've never tried this," she confessed, eyeing the dish uneasily.

"Don't feel bad. They're almost extinct. It's illegal to harvest them in a lot of places: South Africa, Australia, even Washington state."

"Looks like raw chicken."

"Bodega gets all their abalone at Salt Point. The suckers don't make it easy. First you've got to find one hidden among all the seaweed, then you gotta sneak up on it before it torques—twists itself and clings fast to the rocks—and then, hold your breath long enough to pry it loose and bring it to the top."

"Hold your breath? You don't use an air tank?"

He shook his head. "There're strict rules. It's against the law to use scuba to hunt for abalone."

She lowered her nose to her plate to take a cautious sniff. If it smelled like fish, it wasn't fresh. All she could smell though was clean, fresh ocean.

She watched Esteban unroll the cloth napkin, fold it neatly in half across his lap, pick up his knife and fork, and slice one, precise stroke across the raw flesh of his sashimi. It was the simplest of gestures, so why had her lungs stopped working? What was that mysterious sensation inside her? An urgent impatience . . . but for what?

Some women raved about six-packs; others, butts. Savvy had a thing for hands. Bad ones were a deal-breaker. But it wasn't only their shape. Poor grooming was a turnoff too. In her book, not even Joe Manganiello could get away with more than a sliver of white on the tips of his nails.

Worst of all was clumsiness. Watching Esteban, though, there was no ham-handed fisting of his fork, no inept sawing back and forth with his knife. He had the most masculine hands she'd ever seen, yet he used them with the elegance of a dancer. To hell with her prep-school manners. She cocked her head and stared at the ballet on the bar.

With his left hand, he inverted his fork, resting his index finger along its spine as he made another incision. Laying his knife along the plate's edge with a muted clatter, he smoothly transferred the forkful of creamy flesh to his right hand and slid it between white teeth.

"Mm." He closed his eyes, relishing it.

Savvy swallowed along with him, though her mouth was empty. When he opened his eyes and shot her a look of pure pleasure, her heart leapt into her throat.

She gulped again and shifted her gaze to her wineglass to collect herself, though in her mind's eye she still saw *him*. Clearly, Esteban Morales had missed his calling. He should've been a hand model . . . for Tractor Supply Company. Because though he used them with the finesse of a brain surgeon, his hands were super-sized, good for hefting axes or reining draft horses.

He lifted his fork in the next bite, snagging her attention again in spite of herself.

What would it feel like to be touched by hands like that? The whole side of her head would fit in his palm. His fingers could span her waist from rib to hip. The deep ache grew more compelling . . . demanding satisfaction.

"I'll take you there sometime," he was offering.

"Sorry, where?"

"Salt Point."

Now, balanced on his thumb and middle finger, he held out his fork to her mouth. "Here. Taste."

Savvy tensed. *She* wasn't the one who'd ordered raw mollusks. She didn't make snap decisions, especially where vomiting and diarrhea might be involved. She weighed pros and cons, considered costs and benefits. Besides, her appetite for food had dissolved, replaced by a different kind of craving.

In the end, it was the hand that convinced her. How could there be anything bad at the end of those fingers? She remained fixated on it, acutely aware of his eyes intent on her mouth, watching as she closed her lips around the tines while he slowly drew them out. The seafood tasted both sweet and salty, with a scallop-like texture. "Mmmm!"

"I wouldn't lie to you." He took another bite, his gaze still on her mouth. Simultaneously, they savored each other's pleasure . . . the raw flesh melting like lemon butter on their tongues. He lifted his eyes—crinkled at the corners from a life spent outside—to hers in a triumphant grin. The total effect was like sunshine pouring down on her.

Savvy was having way too much fun. Being with Esteban whirled her away into another world, a world without conference tables and briefs. She sucked in a steadying breath. Indulging in frivolous pleasures wasn't the way to reach your goals.

"Go back. Tell me about lavender."

"S'got a ton of potential," he replied easily, while they ate. "Ornamental, for starters. I could sell plants to nurseries or go the direct route, straight to the consumer. Then there's culinary. Everyone's heard of lavender in sweet things like cookies. It makes a great syrup for fruit, with sugar. And it's good in drinks. Now it's being used in place of rosemary and thyme in foods that aren't sweet, too. The most valuable thing, though, is the oil. It's used for perfumes, bug repellent, natural medicine—you name it. But it has to be extracted, and that means investing in equipment . . . learning how to use it."

"Can you make a profit?"

He dabbed his mouth with his napkin, refolded it, and laid it back on his lap while she tried not to stare at those hands.

"It's kind of a rogue industry. It's hard to find good information, especially about wholesale pricing. Technically, there *is* no established lavender industry in the U.S. I've looked at retail prices in catalogs and on websites, and the numbers are all over the place, depending on the quality." He chuckled. "Everyone says theirs is the best, but who knows, when there's no regulation? No standards?"

"There have to be regulations," she said.

He shrugged. "Look it up. If you can find a law about growing lavender somewhere, I'd like to see it."

"I would be very surprised, but anyway—what do you have against grapes?"

"Not a thing, except I only have five acres. Maybe if I had more ground and all the time in the world before I needed to make a profit. Grapes have a long lead time, though. They need a big investment before you see positive returns, let alone payback. Then there's the processing. Who's going to make the wine?"

"You could just sell the grapes to a processor."

"Look." He swigged his beer. "I get what this investment company wants to do. Five more acres tacked on to hundreds already planted in grapes makes perfect sense for them. Not for the little guy like me, though. Besides, there's something about seeing a thing through from start to finish. Like Madre's pepper jelly. I like knowing something went from seed to finished product all on our farm, crafted by our hands."

"This lavender scheme—sounds like it's still a pipe dream." She had to be sure.

He made a face. "I've been experimenting for three years. I'm still looking for the variety that will thrive in our *terreno.*"

She shot the last swallow of wine in her glass. All that was left on their small plates now were the garnishes.

"One-point-six million," said Savvy. "And I need to know by tomorrow."

Chapter 8

"The new offer is six percent over market value," Esteban told his father. They'd just completed their first joint task of the day, partially covering the seed potatoes with soil. Once the plants began to grow, they would continue to fill the trenches as needed until, finally, dirt was mounded up around each vine. Esteban squinted down into the trench. "*Mierda*. I wish this soil wasn't so heavy." Then he looked skyward. "That, or we'd get a long spell of dry weather."

"A good farmer works with the weather the Lord gives him," said Padre. "The spuds did fine when we planted them in this spot three years ago." Potatoes were one of those crops that had to be rotated each year so the nutrients didn't leach out of the soil. "The water will be good for them when the tubers are forming."

"Not when they're trying to cure," countered Esteban.

"They can cure in the field." Potatoes left in the field for a few days of dry weather helped the skins to mature, enabling them to be stored longer. Esteban didn't bother to argue that they'd be curing them in the field anyway, even if the soil was ideal.

Esteban already knew what Padre's decision would be with regard to the increased offer, so why didn't he just come out with it? They were on the same page when it came to the farm. But Padre was the patriarch. It fell to him to lead, and Esteban to follow. Still, he needed some kind of answer for Sauvignon by the end of the day.

When his cell rang toward the end of the drizzly afternoon, he knew who it was without looking.

"Do you have any news for me?" she asked briskly.

She had worked him last night at Bodega. Totally sucked him in with her polite interest in his abalone and her lily of the valley perfume. Then, just when he let his defenses down, she'd T-boned him with the second offer.

Esteban was sowing the spring's first spinach crop, a task he would repeat every ten days during the growing season.

"Not yet," he said, swiping his sleeve across his forehead. "If I were you, I wouldn't get my hopes up."

"I'm coming over."

"Suit yourself." She could camp out in the damn pumpkin patch until Halloween if she thought it would convince Padre to sell, but she'd be wasting her time.

As he slipped his phone back into his jeans, he noticed Padre making his way over to him. Must've heard him talking on the phone.

"Two million dollars," his father said.

"What?"

"You heard me."

"That's half a million more than it's worth!"

Padre straightened up to his full five feet ten inches against his towering son. "Land is worth different things to different people." He held up two fingers. "If they want it, it's two million. Tell them they can take it or leave it." With that, he turned and strode back to his peas.

For the first time, Esteban noticed the slight stoop in his father's spine as he walked away. Padre wouldn't be around forever. A strange surge of protectiveness welled up in him. He raised his voice as high as he dared at Padre's back. "Why are you doing this? You don't want to leave here. Neither does Madre."

But apparently, Padre had already uttered that day's quota of words.

Not long afterward, Esteban heard Savvy's car. He tramped out of the sticky soil toward the lane, in the opposite direction from where Padre had gone.

Last night at Bodega he'd traded his work pants for his good jeans. Today he was back to dressing like the truck farmer that he was. But since there was nothing he could do about looking like a ditch-digger, he distracted himself by wondering what *she* would be wearing today. He'd only ever seen her in drab black. He reached up to pick a pearly pink blossom as he passed by the magnolia tree and twirled it between his fingers and thumb. What would she look like in pink?

He tossed the flower away before he reached the car, letting her open her own door so he didn't defile it with his grimy hand. When she stood before him, all haughty and expectant, he skimmed her over, head to toe.

"Black again. I knew it."

Her mouth tightened into a line and her eyes narrowed to slits. "Hmph," she snorted. "You forgot to mention that in addition to your day job growing beans, you moonlight as a personal shopper."

He couldn't help grinning. "Good one." To his pleasure, her eyes sparkled back at his and she bit back a grin of her own. But not for long.

"So. What's the word?"

He threw up his soiled hands. "I'd invite you into the house to talk, but there's not much sense in it."

She lifted her brow impatiently.

"Our land's not for sale, at any price. Tell your investors not to bother with any more offers."

She raised her chin in defiance. "I'll talk to him." She took a few steps toward the field and his heart leapt into his throat.

"Won't do you any good," he called to her back. She couldn't go out there.

She halted, glancing back with suspicion. "Does your father really not speak English?"

"Nada." Probably understands a helluva lot more than he lets on, though.

"Go ahead then." He gestured far afield to where Padre, the size of a June bug, worked. "Ask him yourself." With studied casualness, Esteban propped his hands on his hips. What would he do if she took him up on it?

She looked down at her good heels. Then up, at the expanse of wet field. Her mouth formed a determined line.

Not selling wasn't an option.

In Savvy's mind's eye, the valley floor transformed itself into the mud-brown carpet in the headmistress's office at Five Oaks Preparatory Academy.

"One-twenty-nine. What a shame," Mrs. Baker said.

Savvy knew what that the test results meant. Mrs. Baker seemed to relish spelling it out, anyway.

"One point too low to be admitted into the gifted program."

Savvy's face burned. She was smart enough. She had to get into that class.

"May I take the test again? I was really tired the first time."
She didn't know that heavy, sleepy feeling was called jet lag. All she knew was she'd do anything to get one-thirty on that test. Back home in California, Papa had been impressed when she'd gotten in to the gifted program. She needed to get into its equivalent here, in Boston. To distinguish herself. Then maybe Papa wouldn't forget about her, out of sight, all the way on the other side of the country.

Mrs. Baker dropped the IQ test into a folder in the back of a file cabinet and rammed the drawer shut. "We can't be repeating tests indefinitely, in hopes you'll eventually score high enough," she said matter-of-factly. She scrawled her signature on some papers and tossed her pen aside.

It wasn't merely recognition Savvy craved. She fingered the folded paper squares hidden in her pocket, letters of desperation from her heartbroken little sisters.

Savvy had memorized Meri's crooked block printing: I hate it here. I don't have any friends.

And Char's tentative cursive: I want to go home. This isn't like my old school. Please, do something.

Savvy was twelve. Old enough to handle anything. Anything, except knowing her sisters were hurting, and not being able to help them. It had been hard enough for Meri and Char when Maman died, let alone hearing all those rumors that Maman had run away from home right before her car crash. And then Papa siding with his lawyers, who'd advised that the best thing would be to send them away . . . away from their homes, their friends, their old schools.

Savvy could take it. But Char and Meri's letters had her worried to the point where she couldn't even eat. After all, Maman had always told her to take care of her little sisters. How could she now though, when she was stuck in Massachusetts, Meri's school was in Rhode Island and Char's, Con-

necticut? Savvy was powerless to help. At least if she got into the gifted program, she could study independently, rush her assignments out of the way, and then work on a plot to get them all back together again. Somehow.

"Come with me," said Mrs. Baker.

Savvy's hands were tied . . . her body, numb. All she could do was follow the headmistress down the hall. When they reached the opening of the plant-filled room where the gifted students roamed freely between microscopes, globes, and shelves full of the classics, Savvy stopped and stared, yearning to be inside. If only she could make Mrs. Baker understand. It wasn't only that she wanted *to be in there. She* needed *to be. To help her sisters.*

"This way," said Mrs. Baker. Next stop: the regular classroom, lined with columns of confining seats. Inquisitive eyes turned to stare, grateful for the least chance to tune out the teacher's drone.

That day Savvy decided to become a lawyer. Lawyers were the guys in suits carrying briefcases who had swooped in to fix things when *Maman* died. Lawyers were smart. They made things happen. If lawyers could convince Papa to send his little girls away, what *couldn't* they do? Once she became a lawyer, she'd never feel powerless again.

Vaguely, she felt the touch of a hand on her elbow. When had Esteban moved to her side, and why was he observing her with concern, as if she were an injured child? As if he saw beyond her tortoiseshell frames, past the somber dress and the carefully arranged bun to the little girl behind the façade, desperate to put her world in order?

"Hey," he said softly. "You can't always get what you want." She heard compassion, not sarcasm in his voice. "Just because Padre doesn't want to sell, it's no reflection on you."

She examined him with mute detachment.

"Do you want me to tell them? Your clients?"

The word *clients* snapped her out of her reverie. "Absolutely not. That wouldn't be appropriate. I'll deal with it." Maybe she couldn't have *everything*, but she was going to get that land for NTI. No way could she fail at her very first assignment.

She studied Esteban in the hazy afternoon light. In his formfitting chambray shirt and faded jeans, with his feet planted firmly on the ground, he was the picture of a simple farmer. Yet this particular farmer was exquisitely made, with the best hands she'd ever seen on a man. Her nostrils flared at his scent, sharper now than it had been last night. At Bodega he'd had the clean smell of soap. Now, at the end of his workday, he smelled earthy, like growing things and sun-warmed soil—the source of all life. Standing next to him made those funny things happen to her insides all over again.

Suddenly she knew what she had to do.

"Sauvignon?"

It was time.

She smiled. "Savvy," she said through lowered lids.

Long past time.

"Call me Savvy."

Something caught his eye over her shoulder, and she turned to see his mother toddling toward them.

"Señorita!" the older woman said, brushing away Savvy's offer of a handshake. "Give me a hug." She pressed her to her pillowy bosom. "I've come to invite you for supper," she announced. "I'm making coq au vin."

"*Coq au vin?*" Her favorite. Jeanne made it at least once a month. Savvy's forehead wrinkled. She could easily imagine Mrs. Morales whipping up a mean batch of empanadas or some spicy mole sauce. But the classic French dish?

Mrs. Morales read her mind. "All you need is an old rooster and some Rioja."

Esteban looked as stunned as Savvy. Still, her mission had just become more complicated and this might help. "I'd love to."

"So you'll come! The rooster is in the pot, and I have salad, fresh from the garden. Everything will be ready in an hour or so."

Savvy brightened. This could fit right in with her plan. "That sounds wonderful. I'll bring something—bread. And wine."

Mrs. Morales clapped her hands with pleasure. "*¡Bueno!* See you at six. Esteban, you and Padre come in and clean up soon." She bustled back toward the house.

"You don't have to come," Esteban told Savvy, after his mother was out of earshot. "Madre always has something on the stove." He patted his stomach. "Must be why I got so big."

"I couldn't turn her down, hurt her feelings. Unless, of course, you have a problem with me coming for dinner . . ."

He shrugged. "Why would I?" There were so many reasons.

"Good." She smiled brightly. "See you in an hour."

Mierda, thought Esteban, watching her walk to her car. In little more than a week, that woman had turned his perfectly ordered life into a perfect shit storm. So why had he felt such concern for her when she got that lost-puppy look, after he told her the land deal was dead? Why couldn't he peel his eyes off her now, as she dodged the rocks, making her way across the spongy ground to her car? Was it his imagination, or did she exaggerate the sway of her hips as she walked? As if she read his sinful mind, she whirled around and shot him one, final smile. *Lost puppy, my ass.* She was a temptress. Maybe Padre was right. The St. Pierres were nothing but trouble.

Now what? For once, he was glad Padre didn't talk much. He didn't want to answer any questions about the way his outrageous counteroffer had been not received, let alone break the news that Savvy St. Pierre was coming for dinner. That was just taking a bath with a toaster. Let Madre take the heat—this was all her idea.

He started for the house, avoiding his father like the plague. He knew Madre had told him when he heard their raised voices from where he was washing up in the bathroom.

"What were you thinking, inviting that woman back into our home? Don't you know sending his daughter over here is a scheme orchestrated by St. Pierre to pilfer our land? You're falling straight into his trap!"

"You're getting too suspicious in your old age, Geraldo. It's not Xavier who is after the farm this time, it's the other investors. *Sauvignon es una chica agradable.* A nice girl. She would never betray us!"

"You've been listening too much to that cook of theirs. Of course she's going to take their side!"

His parents hardly ever yelled. All of this had brought out the worst in Padre. If he found out Esteban had lied to Savvy about his two-million-dollar counteroffer, no telling how he might react.

Esteban toweled his face in the mirror. Sometimes it was a pain in the butt, being bilingual. Sitting down to eat with people who didn't speak the same language wasn't his idea of fun, even when they *didn't* have a history of bad blood. Interpreting was an exercise in rapid-fire decision-making. The slightest nuance might change the entire meaning of a phrase.

He could opt to interpret everything that was said, even if that severely disrupted the normal flow of conversation. On the other hand, if he didn't bother translating at all, he'd catch it from Madre for being disrespectful. That left the middle ground. But where exactly was that? People didn't realize how fast thoughts flew out of their mouths. Or that some thoughts were way harder to translate than others. His head hurt already. Forget about eating—tonight's dinner was a recipe for disaster.

What if both Padre *and* Savvy found out he'd lied about the counteroffer?

And how much did Madre know? She was bilingual too, just didn't often have the confidence to intercede because she hadn't gone to school in America. Had Padre told her he was countering? *¡Mierda!* So much to keep straight! This was what he got for lying.

Chapter 9

Savvy scampered into the kitchen wearing skinny jeans and a baby-blue cashmere sweater with a printed scarf as a belt. "I won't be home for dinner," she announced airily.

Over at the granite-topped island, Jeanne's hand froze above the yellow squash she was slicing. "Who are you? And where is my Sauvignon?"

"What?" Savvy asked, looking down at her outfit. Was she that obvious? She'd always missed having a mother. At her age, though, it felt kind of weird to have another woman hovering over her shoulder. Or maybe she was just afraid Jeanne could read her dirty mind. She was already skittish enough, now that she'd made her decision. "Does a girl have to wear black every day?"

"I thought *you* did," Jeanne replied. "I am amazed that you could find something else, even in a closet the size of a small Caribbean country."

"Hacked from Char," she explained, spinning to give Jeanne the full effect.

"Ah." Her smile faded. She sniffed.

"Jeanne! What's the matter?"

"Nothing, mademoiselle, nothing," said Jeanne, clearing her throat.

Savvy went to her. "Tell me."

Jeanne lowered the hand holding the knife. "It's just . . . in that shade of blue, you look every bit as beautiful as your *maman.*"

Savvy made a sympathetic face and gave her a one-armed hug.

Jeanne wiped her eye with her sleeve. "Where are you going?"

"Next door, to the Moraleses," Savvy replied, snitching a morsel of cheese destined for the squash dish.

"I assume the land negotiations are going well?"

That's all? No comment on the unprecedented fact that she was dining at the home of the opposition?

"We've hit a little glitch. I'm not giving up though. I have a plan."

"That's my girl." As Jeanne worked, her keen eyes flickered over Savvy. "Why is it that your cheeks are so red?"

Savvy flicked a glance into the wall mirror. "Same rouge as ever, must've been a little heavy-handed." She whirled back around, fanning herself. "Do we have any good bread?"

"In my net bag, right there." She motioned with a sticky hand. "I bought extra today."

Savvy reached past Jeanne to withdraw a paper-wrapped baguette from her bag. Then, with a clink, she pulled a bottle of last year's cab from the cooler built into the island.

"Chanel No. 5, yes?" said Jeanne.

Couldn't she get away with anything around here?

Jeanne lifted a knowing brow. "Your dresses are all black, but your scent wardrobe is very diverse. It's a good choice for a date."

"I told you, Jeanne," she said, kissing her cheeks. "It's nothing but business. *À tout à l'heure!*"

She was halfway out of the room when she heard Jeanne's footsteps behind her.

"Wait—I almost forgot. Take this too." She opened a cupboard and withdrew a small glass jar. "A little hostess gift."

The label was in French. "Did you get another package from your sister in Lyon?"

"No. This I sent for special."

"Thanks, Jeanne. You're so thoughtful."

"Give Maria my regards," Jeanne called as Savvy walked out the door.

"I will. Oh, and Jeanne, could you do me a favor when you see Char?"

Jeanne lifted a brow.

"Remind her I said we need to sit down and talk about her prenup."

Esteban listened for the slam of Savvy's car door. He needed to catch her before she set foot in the house, to lay the ground rules. *First and foremost, don't talk about the offer on the land.*

Too late. By the time he got back from the living room carrying a flimsy, straw-bottomed chair that he prayed wouldn't collapse under his weight, she was already standing on the other side of the glass, hand poised to knock.

"Is that Señorita Sauvignon? Tell her to come in!" said Madre.

But his mouth wouldn't work. That blue sweater had struck him speechless. All he could do was hold the door open and try not to gape as she sashayed across the threshold.

She had breasts. Two of them. Peach-sized, by his estimation. They'd gone completely unnoticed earlier, beneath those dreary nun habits.

She handed Madre a skinny loaf of bread, a bottle of red wine, and a yellowish jar, and the two women reunited as if they hadn't seen each other for sixty years instead of sixty minutes, kissing, laughing, and chirping like a couple of magpies.

Padre rode in from the living room on a wave of palpable suspicion, quieting the women, making Esteban's muscles tense up tighter than a gnat's ass. When Savvy turned to Padre with a look of open curiosity, Esteban remembered with a start that they'd not yet been formally introduced. If he'd had his way, they never would be. Worrying about keeping his stories straight had him so stressed he couldn't wait for dinner to be over, and it hadn't even started yet. How was he going to think clearly with that sweater sitting across from him?

"Padre, this is Sauvignon."

"Savvy," she said respectfully. "Nice to meet you, sir."

Padre nodded curtly and took the hand she offered.

There was the scrape of chairs as everyone took their seats. After only a few days, Savvy was starting to look right at home in Esteban's usual spot.

Madre set her pot in the center of the table and told everyone to help himself.

"Smells wonderful!" said Savvy, ladling broth into her bowl.

In Spanish, Padre said the blessing, picked up his spoon, and paused, frowning. "What is this?" he grumbled.

"Es pollo en vino," replied Madre matter-of-factly.

"En treinta y ocho años de matrimonio, nunca has hecho pollo como esta." In forty-one years of marriage, you have never made chicken like this.

A hush fell over the room. Esteban and Savvy stilled, eyeing his parents uneasily.

"It's French. I made it in honor of Señorita Savvy," Madre replied, serving herself last. "And even if you don't like it, you will eat it anyway, so as not to make a fool of yourself in front of our guest."

Esteban groaned inwardly. *Off to a great start—*

"It's a sad state of affairs when a man is told what to do in his own house," Padre groused in Spanish.

Smiling brightly, Madre turned to Savvy. "He says, it looks delicious."

From the edge of his rickety seat, Esteban waited with bated breath as Padre mouthed his first spoonful of the stew.

Savvy tore a hunk of bread from the baguette. "Here, Mr. Morales . . ."

Esteban cringed. *Don't make it worse!*

"I brought you some . . ." She stopped short, gaze flickering helplessly between Esteban and Madre.

Padre was used to rolled up tortillas, not doughy French bread. . . .

"Pan," said Madre. *"Pan* is bread in Spanish."

"Pan." Savvy smiled and nodded encouragingly, tempting Padre like a dog with a bone.

Though he eyed it suspiciously, Padre finally accepted her offering. *"Gracias."* He dipped the bread into his broth. When he'd eaten it, he tore another hunk off the loaf.

Esteban and his mother sighed with relief. The ice had been broken.

Madre's gift of gab took it from there. Crazy how two women who were poles apart in age, nationality, and class could find so much to talk about, yet their shared interests seemed to go on forever. Vegetables, roses, weather, cooking—after a while Esteban lost track. He'd almost let his guard down enough to actually *taste* his second helping of chicken when Padre's hand went to his obliques in a gesture that was becoming more and more familiar lately.

"His back again," said Madre in English. In Spanish, she said to him, "I made another batch of oregano oil. I'll rub some on your back later on."

"That's too bad," Savvy said. "I don't mean to interfere, but wouldn't it give you peace of mind to know Mr. Morales wouldn't have to keep working forever? If only he would consider reopening negotiations on your property . . ." She took an innocent sip from her bottle of Coke.

Padre looked up sharply, his spoon falling to his empty flan plate with a clatter. He scowled inquiringly at Esteban, prompting new concern on Madre's face.

"Señorita Savvy says she's glad you're keeping an open mind with regard to negotiations," Esteban told his father.

"What do you mean, an open mind? Didn't you give her my counteroffer?"

"That was only this afternoon. Give her time to present it."

Padre grunted. "Tell her to take all the time she needs. No one is *loco* enough to pay that much money."

"What did he say?" asked Savvy.

"He said he'll think about it," replied Esteban.

Savvy smiled.

"Well!" said Madre. "If everyone is finished . . ." She rose to whisk away the empty pot. Esteban and Savvy carried their own plates to the sink, where he picked up the small jar Savvy had brought.

"Lavender honey, from France," said Savvy.

Esteban opened the lid, touched the honey's surface with a finger and licked it off. "What kind of lavender?" He studied the foreign print on the label.

"I don't know. Jeanne sent away to Provence for it."

"That Jeanne . . . so thoughtful. Give her my thanks," said Madre. "Esteban, did you tell Savvy about your lavender?"

"*Sí.*"

¡Mierda! When he was nervous, he slipped into Spanish. He hated being tagged as an immigrant . . . hated worse the fact that he hated it. Once he had kids of his own, they'd be rid of that stigma—born Americans. But the fact that he was bilingual wasn't news. He'd been acting as an interpreter—if a dishonest one—for the past hour.

"Has she seen your experiments?"

"Madre. I doubt she's interested in—"

"What experiments?" asked Savvy.

"Go out and show her the greenhouse," said Madre, dismissing them with a wave. "Go on. I'll take care of these few dishes."

Savvy tilted her head and smiled. "I've always had a thing for greenhouses. So many interesting scents."

He was such a sucker. She'd probably never been in a greenhouse in her life. But Madre had been prompting him to be more outgoing since he was a shy little kid. She knew if there was anything he could open up about, it was lavender.

"Let's go," he said, leading the way.

Chapter 10

For the first time in days, no clouds smudged the evening sky, only a sliver of new moon glowing in the dusk.

Savvy fairly skipped along in the cool evening air, trying to keep up with Esteban's long strides. She wanted to kiss Mrs. Morales, first for the chance to finally meet her husband and now to be alone with her son.

A dense wall of humidity hit her the moment she stepped inside the glass-paned building. She inhaled in stages, the thick, fragrant air heavy in her lungs.

"I love the smell of healthy, growing things. My friends thought I was weird, but I used to hang out in the greenhouse at college sometimes. Even took an Intro to Botany course for one of my electives, junior year." She winced at her lame attempt at small talk. What did Esteban care about her college courses? The whole time she'd had her nose buried in Evolution and Speciation, he'd been planted right here, studying this slip of land by the feel of the soil in his fingers, learning about the seasons by watching the sky.

But he wasn't unreceptive. "What's it smell like to you?"

"A million things, all at once . . ." She belly-breathed, trying to break down the complex aroma into its individual components. "Like the color green. Do smells have color, to you? You know. Sharp . . . metallic . . ."

"That's the magnesium in the chlorophyll."

He picked up a pair of garden clippers with curved blades lying on a shelf.

A long trough of gray-green plants with narrow, toothed leaves ran down the center of the greenhouse. They seemed to be color-coded by their blossoms, ranging from pink through lilac and violet blue to deep purple.

Esteban snipped off a sprig of dusky blue violet and held it under her nose. "Describe this one to me."

Savvy loved a challenge. "A potent musk and . . . camphor?"

He nodded. "*Lavandula angustifolia*. True English lavender."

He moved down the row to some light blue flowers. "How about this?"

"Um, more rosemary-ish." She lit up with sudden recognition. "Like the stuff Celine sprays on our sheets!" Immediately, she wanted to go curl up in a corner of the greenhouse and die. He was a *farmer*, for the love of God. Not everyone was lucky enough to sleep on perfumed sheets.

He let it slide. "Lavandula Goodwin Creek Grey. Good container plant."

"Let me pick one," she said eagerly. People in the industry said Papa had a phenomenal nose for blending wines. Savvy had always been pretty good at deciphering scents, too.

Esteban passed her the clippers, warm from his hand. "Go for it."

She chose a long spike of deep violet flowers soaring above compact foliage. "Wow!" Her head flew backward. "Soft and sweet, yet at the same time, pungent."

Esteban grinned. "That's *Lavandula x intermedia Grosso*—lavandin for short. Sounds better than 'grosso.'" He grinned sideways. "Some people think it's the most fragrant strain. But it's a mule—a hybrid. It can't reproduce." He gave her an appreciative look. "You have a good sense of smell, did you know that?"

"Papa says I inherited that from him."

He hid all three cuttings behind his back. "Close your eyes."

She did as she was told, excited to play.

"Is this the first, second, or third stem I cut?"

"Third."

"Okay. How about this one."

"First."

"Maybe your Papa is right."

"Ha!" she said happily. "Now it's your turn."

"It's a waste of time. I live with these plants." He swept one long arm across the rows. "I can pick out every one of these blindfolded."

"Oh really? Let's see about that." Brazenly, she tugged on the knot of her scarf-slash-belt.

His eyes flew open in mild surprise. "You don't trust me?"

"I'm a lawyer. I don't trust anybody." She gave him an impish grin. "Turn around." Though she was five-seven, taller than the average woman, she still had to reach up high to flip the slippery silk over his eyes and tie it at the back of his head, careful not to get his shoulder-length black hair caught in the knot.

Then she took him by the upper arms, spinning him until he stood straight and tall as an oak tree before her. But while he might have the edge when it came to size, she could *see*. It occurred to her that she could scrutinize him hard as she wanted now, starting at the top . . . moving down. Like she'd done with the David in the Academia. She shivered with a secret thrill.

Beneath the blindfold, his nose was a little too prominent to be considered classic, but his full lower lip more than made up for it. That untamed look, the farmer tan, and his rock-hard body added up to more than the sum of its parts. From the moment she'd met him, there had never been a time when she hadn't been acutely aware of Esteban's merest movement, even on that very first day, the day she'd killed Marlena . . .

Her fingers furled and unfurled at her sides, itching to touch his clean-shaven cheek. *Not yet.* She'd held out for this long. Now, knowing the drought would soon end, she basked in anticipation. Besides, she'd only inspected the tip of the iceberg. Decadently, she let her eyes languish farther south, to the red plaid cotton shirt that stretched over muscular shoulders. Pearl-covered snaps lined up where stodgy buttons ought to have been. One quick yank, and—

Soon.

A glint off his belt buckle caught her eye—but not for long. Much more intriguing was the denim-clad area beneath it, deep navy in the fold, fading to cornflower where the fabric bulged outward. Her lips parted and she became aware of her chest rising and falling with her breath. There it was again—that persistent, demanding yearning . . . for what? She knew the facts of life. But knowing something wasn't the same as experiencing it. She'd always been too busy studying. Working. Excelling. Now, though, she was almost ready. A syrupy warmth infused her stomach and spiraled downward.

"Well?" He raised his gorgeous hands—the ones she'd had to concentrate on not staring at all through dinner with his parents—in a shrug, unwittingly showing off the delectable hollows in the center of his palms. Her smallish breasts would hardly fill them up. She hoped she wouldn't disappoint.

Not now. Not tonight . . .

"What are you waiting for?"

She'd totally lost track of which sample of lavender was which. She stuck a random cutting under his nose.

. . . but soon.

"Easy. Lavandin," he said.

"Wrong!" She held out a different flower, biting her lip to keep from giggling.

"Again."

Savvy had always been a good girl. A rule follower. Who knew being mischievous could be so much fun?

Above her scarf, his forehead wrinkled in a frown. "That's . . . one more time."

She waved yet another, random sample, and he gave it a sniff.

"You're cheating." His hands went toward the blindfold.

"Nonononono!" Her pent-up laughter spilled out and she held down his forearms, impressed by their ropy firmness. "Don't take it off yet. I'll play fair. I promise."

But wild impulses hijacked her intentions. Here he was, her very own David. Her blind captive, to do with as she pleased. How could she resist?

Before she could change her mind, she went up on her toes, slipping her hand around the curve of his neck beneath the fall of his hair. In the second before he caught on, it was like hugging a surprised tree trunk. Then he became malleable, letting her take the lead, passively allowing his head to be guided down to where she pressed her closed lips to his.

She hadn't been expecting him to turn the tables. What had been putty in her hands seconds earlier abruptly hardened into to decisive, capable *male*.

With one mighty arm, Esteban hauled her into his chest, while his other hand cradled the back of her head. His mouth opened over hers, his tongue delved into her . . . and she was gone. Swept away . . . her heart slamming against her chest, her pulse rocketing out of control.

Had she really thought she could tease this earthy man with no repercussions?

His eyes were still blinded, while hers were fastened on him, watching him dive in to ravish her again and again with his mouth, his everywhere-hands taking possession of her. They spanned her lower back, pressing her into him with a controlled power that made her gasp. Breathlessly, she stared over his shoulder at a wall of green while his fingers fumbled in her chignon, extracting her bobby pins, scattering them without a care. Once her hair flowed free, he wrapped it around his fist like a rope and used it to gently force her head back, giving him access to plaster a row of kisses down her neck.

She bet he'd been kissing women for ages.

A low scraping sound in his chest filled her with an unsettling heat. Panic mingled with pleasure.

Seducing Esteban had begun as business stratagem, a means to an end. But it wasn't turning out as planned. Unexpectedly, she felt like the victim, not the perpetrator.

Why should she care? Was she naïve enough to think that she was his first? She doubted there were too many twenty-seven-year-old men around who still had their V-cards. Besides, this wasn't about love. It was about trading favors while checking off a necessary item from her to-do list.

The atmosphere thickened as his breath came faster, heavier. His hand had released her hair and was on the back of her head again, tilting it to give him better access. Sensations crowded out thoughts. She grew dizzy with the oppressive heat of the surroundings, the cloying, almost hypnotic smell of grassy musky blossoms, the feel of his hands on her body . . . until she felt hard plastic slip from her temples and hit the gravel with a soft *ssshht.*

"My glasses!" Reflexively, her hands flew up, flailing at the air like a mime's against the side of an imaginary box.

Esteban whipped off his blindfold.

"Help me find my glasses!"

Everyone who knew Savvy knew not to mess around when it came to her glasses. Even Char and Meri had learned, at a very young age, that the "most-rational" sister turned into an instant crazy person if one of them dared to play hide-and-seek with her "eyes." Without them, she was virtually blind.

Unfortunately, Esteban did not know her that well yet.

Vaguely, she saw him—or a shape that might be him—stoop, and then rise.

"Did you find them?" she cried.

"Got 'em."

Frantically, she clawed at the clammy air. "Where are they? Give them to me!"

"In my pocket."

"Give them to me! I can't see!"

"Oh, so it's okay for me to be blind, but not you?" he asked calmly. Logically.

This was no time for logic. She lunged in the direction of his front pockets, but he caught her wrists.

"Tu es hermosa," he breathed, transferring both her wrists to one of his hands, bringing them to the center of her pounding chest.

"You're okay," he whispered. "I won't hurt you."

Her arms relaxed a little.

Tenderly, he planted a kiss on one cheek, then the other. He stroked her loose hair with his free hand. "I've been imagining what you looked like without those things."

He bunched up her hair next to her ear, then fanned it out and let it fall. "You look completely different this way." This time, when he kissed her, the already pleasant familiarity was a comfort, not threat. *"Una mujer*—a woman—not a lawyer."

Objection. She'd fought long and hard for her professional persona. No one was invited behind that mask, other than family, thank you very much.

Gradually, his kisses began to prod again. When he found that she tolerated, even welcomed, them, they became darker, more insistent. He cast her wrists away finally and reached around with both hands to cup her rear end, pressing her into his hardness.

Without sight, Savvy's other senses were heightened. The atmosphere in the greenhouse was like a steam room. The heady smell of lavender filled her deprived lungs to bursting. All she could see was his blurry outline in a sea of green. All she could hear was the sound of his voice, softly murmuring in Spanish.

"Mía."

Her mind swirled and twirled. . . . She couldn't get enough air. . . . She was going to faint. What did *mía* mean?

He was sliding his hand under the back of her sweater and moving it around to cover one bra cup with an all-encompassing heat and—

What did she think she was she doing?

"Wait. Stop," she said, panicked. She was supposed to be the seducer here, not the seducee! She'd wanted to overwhelm *him*. She hadn't counted on losing control herself.

Immediately, Esteban obeyed, dropping his hands, though his feet remained rooted in place.

Savvy staggered backward, yanking down her sweater.

"I—it's time for me to go. And before I do, I have to—thank your mother. Tell your parents good-night," she managed to get out between blind, breathless gasps.

She licked her raw lips and held out a trembling hand. "Now," she demanded in her best courtroom voice. "Give. Me. My—"

A vague shape came toward her face. She felt the profound relief of the stems being guided over her ears.

When the world came back into focus, the confused disappointment on Esteban's face triggered a stab of guilt in Savvy's core.

David-like hands safely at his sides, his eyes locked into hers as she stood there, panting.

"Just one thing," he whispered. "Who's doing the experimenting here? Me? Or you?"

Without answering, Savvy whirled around to the direction of the exit and hurried out of the sweltering heat. As soon as she got outside, she stopped and leaned a hand against the glass to catch her breath. She'd expected to hear his footsteps behind her, but to her disappointment, he'd done as she'd asked. Stopped.

Chapter 11

Esteban fingered a flower on the scarf he held. He brought it to his nose to smell Savvy's perfume, then stuffed it into his back pocket. Who *was* the chameleon who lived next door? A cold, conniving lawyer who'd do anything to cut a deal? A cock-teasing wine princess? Or an innocent *chica?*

He meandered among the comforting familiarity of his precious plants, checking moisture levels, taking note of comparable degrees of bloom, giving her time to say her good-byes to his parents and himself time to recover before locking up the greenhouse for the night. He'd so hoped that this would be the year one of these strains would take root outside the protected environment of the greenhouse, in the truck gardens. So far, it didn't look good.

After a while, he stepped out into the cool night.

When he reached the house, Madre sat in her woven lawn chair on the narrow front porch, an old serape thrown around her shoulders. A cat weaved in and out of her ankles.

"Esteban. Is everything okay?"

"What are you doing, sitting out here in the dark?"

"I always sit out on the porch in the evenings."

"In the summer. It's only March."

"What happened with Señorita?"

He was a grown-ass man. Was he supposed to report to his *mami* every time he kissed a woman?

"Nothing." He started toward the front door.

"Then why was her hair all messed up when she came in to say good-night?"

He halted mid-step. "Nothing you need to worry about."

"Tell me what's going on. At supper, Padre says he's waiting for an answer on his counteroffer, and Señorita doesn't know anything about a new offer. Why do you pit them against each other?"

Esteban sat down in the chair that was Padre's and rested his elbows on his knees, grateful it was dark. Hanging out on the porch was characteristic of his parents' generation, something an immigrant might do.

"It wasn't a lie. Padre made an offer that no one would accept. It's just another way of saying he doesn't want to sell."

"How do you know this offer is too much?"

"Two million dollars? No one's going to spend that much money on this property."

Madre was no expert on real estate. She couldn't argue. "What about you, son? Do you want to stay here?"

He'd never considered that question before, and now it had come up twice within days. There'd always been an understanding: the son would take over for the father. To reject that was to reject everything. He owed it to his family to continue the *Plan Familiar*. What other choice did he have? He was lucky to be here, even if sometimes he felt like just a cog in the wheel.

"Mami. Don't talk like that."

"I'm hearing your words, but I'm not feeling them here"—she tapped her substantial breast—"in my heart."

Had he upset her? Maybe he hadn't grown up rich, but he'd always known he was loved. He had a deep appreciation for all his parents had given him. He didn't want to disappoint them. "Yes, I want to stay here. Maybe not do everything *exactly* like Padre . . ." Even that small concession felt epic, for a family as tied to tradition as theirs. "But yes."

They sat in silence for a moment, listening to the peepers down by the creek.

"Let me ask you something."

Madre rocked and waited.

"Whatever happened between Padre and Xavier St. Pierre?"

She looked out into the night. "It was so long ago, I can hardly remember. There was a meeting in town. All the growers, big and small, were there. It started out Señor St. Pierre and your *padre* were on the same side. But after the meeting, they got into a argument over who was first to bring winegrapes to the valley. St. Pierre said the

French. Padre asked how he could forget it was Spanish monks who introduced grape vines to California, long before the French."

Esteban opened his palms. "And?"

"That's it."

"That's *it?* Two decades of bad blood over *that?*"

"That's what I told you. In the beginning, it was nothing. But you know how bullheaded your Padre can be. Must be, Señor St. Pierre is the same way. Neither one can let it go."

Esteban shook his head in disbelief. He vowed never to become that stubborn.

"Maybe it's a growing-up lesson for you. The past is important. But it's not good to get stuck in the past by pride. Better to move forward."

He turned to examine his mother. He'd thought she was all about the past. She certainly led her life in the traditional way, going along with whatever Padre wanted.

"How is the lavender today?"

He scrubbed his hand over his face, suddenly bone-tired. "I'll find one that works sooner or later. Soon as it dries out."

He rose and stretched. "*Buenas noches,* Mami. Thanks for supper. It was good."

Lying on his side in his bedroom, his feet hanging off his mattress, he couldn't stop staring at the limp heap of Savvy's scarf on his nightstand.

He'd told her "no more offers." What if Savvy took his lie to heart and he never heard from her again? Was he fated to remember her by the few times she'd warmed his kitchen chair? The sight of her perfect oval face behind her dorky glasses? The feel of the material covering her peach-like breasts, never knowing the real thing?

What had he expected? *Cristo,* she was Sauvignon St. Pierre. Did he really think he, an immigrant truck farmer, could ever matter to her?

He rolled over to keep from seeing the nightstand, kicking at his tangled sheets in frustration. He had to see her at least one more time. That scarf was his ticket.

Chapter 12

Savvy had to see Esteban again.

She lay in her California king bed studying the morning shadows flickering across the carved plaster rosette in the ceiling, for once glad that it was Saturday and she didn't have to go to work.

She needed a plan. She'd almost blown it last night, freaking out over the loss of her glasses, rejecting his embraces after throwing herself at him.

She turned her face into her fat feather pillow to muffle her humiliated groan. She was so blessed—a good education and all the advantages that came with a moneyed upbringing. When it came to men, though, she didn't have a clue. It was easier to keep her eye on the business aspect of this.

No more offers. That's what he'd said. But no didn't mean no. It just meant she had to find another way to yes. And she had the perfect plan . . . even if her skill set to implement it left something to be desired.

She reached for her phone on her nightstand, fell back on her pillow, and Googled lavender, getting a zillion hits. So she narrowed it down to lavender farms, narrowed *that* to lavender farms in Northern California. Those results, she could count on one hand. And none of those farms allowed visitors except during special events.

But some growers utilized local retailers to sell their products. She clicked on some links, and *bingo. Savvy St. Pierre, you are a genius.*

A store called Smells Like Napa specialized in—what else?—oils, lotions, potpourri, and other so-called hyper-local products. An ideal place to learn more about Esteban's favorite herb, not to mention envelop herself in that indescribable scent again.

While they were at the store, she would let Esteban know in no uncertain terms that she was ... *available.* She shivered with anticipation. Now that she had the venue, she had to get herself ready.

She sat straight up in bed and threw off the covers. It was going to feel weird asking for her sisters' advice when usually it was the other way around. If there was anything both Char and Meri were both expert in, though, it was clothes.

Her fingers flew across her phone's keypad. NEED WARDROBE AD-VICE. She paused, then added: FOR A DATE. Then she started counting. *One, two ...*

Within ten seconds, Meri and Char were falling all over each other to see who could get through her bedroom door first.

"You did it!" said Char.

"A date? You mean like, a real date?" Meri bounced onto Savvy's bed.

Char joined them among the rumpled blankets. "I was talking to Ry when I got the text," she told Meri. "Frankly, I was starting to wonder if she even liked boys."

"Who is he? C'mon, tell us! We're dying here!"

Savvy hugged her pillow, unable to suppress her mile-wide grin.

"You're never going to guess."

Meri flung a throw pillow toward Savvy's head and she blocked it in the nick of time. "All right, all right," she laughed. "Are you ready?" She drew the wait out a few seconds more. "Esteban Morales."

Her sisters sat there in stunned disbelief.

"Who's—wait, *Esteban Morales?*" repeated Meri.

"The Esteban Morales who lives next door?" asked Char with a shocked expression.

Savvy lifted her shoulders, looking from one to the other, her grin even wider, if that was possible.

Her sisters' words tumbled over each other. "What the heck! Do we even *know* Esteban Morales? I mean, *know him* know him?"

"You remember the guy I was talking to at Bodega the other night?"

"That was Esteban Morales?" they said in chorus.

"Why didn't you tell us then that he was the Esteban from next door?"

"I told you his name was Esteban."

"There are lots of Estebans in California. You failed to mention it was *that* one. He is one hot tamale! How did you two meet?" asked Char.

"How do I meet anyone? Business."

Meri rolled her eyes. "Surprise, surprise. Come on. Tell us about this date."

"He's really into growing lavender. Trying to learn as much about it as he can. So, I found this shop that I want to take him to."

"Wait, *you* asked *him* out?"

"*Going to* ask. Not asked."

"He doesn't know yet?"

"No. I just decided, about five minutes ago."

"Okaaaay . . ."

"Isn't this a little . . . *sudden?* I mean, for you? When was the last time you were with a guy? "

There was no good answer for that. "So which one of you has the perfect outfit that I can borrow?"

Meri and Char looked at each other with puzzled expressions. Most sisters were always in each other's closets. Not hers.

"What's the big deal? You just pull on a—oh, yeah." Meri straightened, recalling Savvy's conservative everyday style. "I told you you needed some color in your closet, for this very reason."

"Sorry. I don't plan *my* love life around *your* taste."

"You don't have a love life," Meri snarkily pointed out.

"Ha," Savvy said. "If I did, I wouldn't plan it around your taste."

Char jumped up. "I know!" she said, sounding like an over-enthusiastic kindergarten teacher. "Let's go take a look in my closet first. I'm sure there's something that'll work. It's unanimous: anything's better than head-to-toe black."

A dozen outfits later, with half of Char's extensive wardrobe spilling across her bed onto the carpet, Meri shared her thoughts from where she lounged sideways across a slipper chair, one foot swinging back and forth.

"I think we're done here. Char, no offense, but your stuff falls into two categories. Lululemon, and Kate Middleton-ish. Savvy's credibility would be trashed if we let her out of the house in those itty-bitty short-shorts you favor—"

"They're called competition briefs, and everyone wears them to run," Char said in self-defense.

"—and all these Jenny Packham dresses are precious, but . . ." She sprang to her feet, grabbed Savvy's hand, and led her out of Char's room. "C'mon. I've got some ideas."

A minute later, Savvy stood before her artist sister's open closet door. "Looks like a rainbow threw up in here."

Meri cut in front of her, scraping hanger after hanger across the bar. "Now *this* is what you call a wardrobe. There's frockage here for every occasion."

"Ah! Here we are. DVF wrap dress. Prim, yet flattering."

Savvy pursed her lips to the side. "Can we not do a print? I'm already stepping out of my comfort zone here."

Meri shoved the dress back onto the rod. "How about this?" She held up what looked like a purple fabric Popsicle.

"That's a dress?"

Meri took a second look. "Hm. Maybe not."

Char said, "You could just wear my jeans again."

Meri's eyes widened with horror. Holding up her palms for emphasis, she said, "No jeans!"

"You love jeans," said Savvy.

"There's a place for them, but this isn't it. This is your first date in probably forever!"

Savvy was feeling less, well, *savvy* by the second. She sighed, pulling her black knit pajamas back on over the underwear she'd donned for the try-ons, and plopped down onto the edge of Char's bed. "I think I'm going to have to go shopping. Like, real shopping. To an actual *store.*"

What she *didn't* say was that the past hour had shown her there was something else she needed besides an outfit. She'd caught the mirrored reflection of her standard-issue beige bra and panties from every possible angle. While perfectly functional for preventing panty lines under her work clothes, they weren't exactly . . . provocative. She could never tell her sisters that, though. She'd be humiliated beyond words if they caught on to her real plan. Besides, it was her job to protect them, not corrupt them.

Meri tossed her thick mahogany mane. "Might as well. You're going to want all new underwear, anyway."

Savvy's head whipped around. Were her thoughts that transparent?

Char yawned. "She's right. Don't want to be caught unprepared in those geriatric granny panties—not that I doubt you have some perfectly lovely, feminine ones, stashed in the back of a drawer somewhere."

Geriatric? All Savvy's underwear was like that. Bought in bulk for her new job. Her face warmed. How could her sisters—her *younger* sisters—be so blasé about sex? What would they think if they knew she'd never "done it"? It was getting ridiculous. She was twenty-seven. Both her sisters had recently found the loves of their lives and were deliriously happy. They were probably doing it like rabbits. And here she was, well on her way to becoming a shriveled-up old prune.

"Of course. New underwear. That's a given. Fuchsia. Or red, or purple or something . . ." She popped up. "I'd better get going. See you guys later."

"Do you want us to go with you?" asked Char.

"That's sweet of you. So sweet." Savvy smiled with gratitude. "But no. No need. I can do this on my own." There was other stuff she needed to buy, too. And she sure as heck didn't want company for that. It would be hard enough to do without their prying, pitying eyes.

Meri looked doubtful. "Send us fitting-room pics on your phone if you're undecided."

"We're here for you," added Char.

Except wasn't Char usually somewhere with Ryder, of late? And Meri, with Mark?

As Savvy walked back to her room, she turned to see the concern on their faces. She couldn't have her little sisters preoccupied, worrying about her. That wasn't how it was supposed to be.

"Don't worry!" she called. "I'll be fine!"

Savvy paid for her white lacy underthings—feminine yet in no way, heaven forbid, slutty—and added the tissue-filled shopping bag to the stack on her arm. After an exhausting day in fitting rooms, she'd finally settled on a green dress—fun and flirty—with a zip back. A breeze to slip out of.

One stop left. Best to go to a CVS here, in San Francisco, instead of the one in Napa. She'd die if she ran into anyone she knew!

She headed for the magazine section and leafed through the whole May issue of *Elle*, a *Vogue*, and half a *Marie Claire* waiting for the wall o' condoms in front of the pharmacy counter to empty of customers. Why did they have to stock the condoms in the busiest part of the store? At last, checking over her shoulder, she tiptoed toward that wall. *Holy crap.* The choices were overwhelming. Should she get Thin or Ultra Thin? Ribbed? Lubricated? Double-ecstasy? *Vibrating?* And what about size? Most of what they stocked was XL. For the love of God, not every man could be an XL. Was that only to build up guys' egos? Or had the store sold out of the smaller sizes? What exactly would happen if a woman handed her man a mere medium-sized condom? *"Sorry, honey, I estimated the best I could."* Was that automatic grounds for a breakup?

And what was all the fuss about latex? Might Esteban be allergic? Might *she?* Talk about embarrassing—breaking out in a hideous rash, right in the middle of things.

Furtively, she snatched up an armful of random boxes and hoped for the best. After paying the jaded clerk, who never even made eye contact, she hurried to her car.

Behind the steering wheel, she whooshed out a relieved breath. *Mission accomplished.* She stuffed the plastic CVS bag into her Nordstrom shopper so the cop wouldn't see it, in the off-off chance she got pulled over. Then she shifted into drive and went back out on the freeway.

Now all she had to do was inform Esteban that they had a date.

She pulled up her planner. This week was going to be a doozy. She was scheduled to be in court starting Tuesday, assisting one of the partners in a complicated jury trial. Who knew what time she'd get out each day or when the case would end? They were up against a top-notch legal team from the city. The trial might even run into next week. To be safe, she chose Wednesday for the date—a week and four days away. Farther out than she wanted, but maybe it wasn't so bad. She didn't want to seem overeager. Not only that, it would give her more time to get her nerve up. Already she was a wreck, contemplating what it was she was about to do.

Funny. Amid all her preparations, she kept thinking more about Esteban and less about the land deal. And not just his awesome hands and god-like body, though those images were never far from her mind as she tried on dress after dress, judging them by the ease with which they could be whisked off her willing body.

She'd also thought more about his family story. How his parents had been farsighted enough to give up everything in their homeland so that Esteban would have his own stake here in America. About Mr. Morales's tidy rows of vegetables and Mrs. Morales's kind, generous heart.

Don't get all warm and fuzzy, Savvy. Keep your eye on the prize.

She was going to seduce Esteban into revisiting the land sale. She couldn't let sentimental musings get in the way of that. After all, she had no illusions about a long white gown or a picket fence. No ... all her fantasies were centered around a sign on her desk that said SAUVIGNON ST. PIERRE, followed by the word PARTNER. Finally catching up with every other twenty-seven-year-old in the country in terms of sex was only a bonus.

Esteban could cut another slash in his bedpost. Wasn't that all guys cared about?

His parents could quit busting their hind ends and start enjoying their golden years.

There's a word for women who use their bodies to get ahead. Was Savvy really so bad, though? In the end, it was a win-win for everyone.

Case closed.

Chapter 13

At eleven-fifteen on Sunday, Esteban texted Savvy:
YOU LEFT YOUR SCARF HERE.

A few minutes later, his phone rang.

"Esteban! Hi! I'm so glad you found my scarf. Listen, I have an idea that you might like. At least, I like it, which is why I thought you would. Have you ever heard of a place called Smells Like Napa?"

For a lawyer, she sounded awfully nervous. Hyper, even.

"No."

"It's a retail outlet for local herb growers. They sell all kinds of products, from the herbs themselves to essential oils and anything else you could imagine. Yeah. So, anyway, I was wondering if you might want to go there together sometime, poke around, see what they're about, what they have? I mean, if you have time. I know you have an awful lot of work to do."

"Sure."

"Really?"

"When?"

"I'm going to be super busy with a case for the next week and a half. Is the Wednesday after next okay? And then I can get my scarf from you at the same time."

"Wednesday's good for the store. But I'm on my way to give you your scarf now."

"Now?"

"You only live a few hundred yards from here."

"Great! Okay then. Why not? You could come over now. I just got home from church and I'm not doing anything. Important, that is. It's Sunday. Day of rest and all that."

"Great. See you in a few."

"See you!"

Women. Why did they have to make everything so complicated?

A text from one of his diving buddies had come in while he was talking.

Conditions primo at SP winds below 10, seas under 6 & > 10 apart

NorCal divers waited for the first day of abalone season like kids waiting for Christmas. Esteban considered the data: clear and sunny with calm seas, excellent for hunting abalone. This time of year, though, the water was bound to be freezing. He shivered, imagining about how it would feel with the Pacific Ocean seeping into his wet suit.

Still, soon the farmers' market would open and most of his weekends would be tied up until October. Besides, when wasn't it cold at Salt Point? He calculated the drive time. Thirty minutes to load up the Chevy and drop off Savvy's scarf, then another thirty to get to Shane's. He texted back:

Pick u up at 12:15

Since he'd gotten into diving, Esteban had met divers from towns miles apart, up and down the coast. A few were even from Napa. Like Hector, who'd been a couple of years ahead of Esteban at Vintage High. Hector wasn't his best bud—he had already been out working before Esteban graduated—but he was cool. Last year they'd run into Hector's cousin, Shane, when they were up at Salt Point. Shane lived right off Route 1, on the way to the coast. After that, Esteban had given Shane a ride a couple of times.

He dug his wet suit and dive gear from out of the back of his closet and tossed them into the truck bed, along with some old beach towels, water bottles, and a couple of ice chests.

Esteban slowed his pickup as it crunched down the white gravel driveway of Domaine St. Pierre. When he got close to the sprawling mansion, he peered up through the windshield at it. Though he could see the estate through the trees from his backyard, the Moraleses' homestead might as well be on the other side of the world. Here, he was surrounded by professionally manicured gardens tended by *braceros*. No secret, Mexicans made up more than half the work force of the valley. A tower of water tumbled down from a fountain that formed a traffic circle in the middle of the St. Pierre drive. He wondered if Savvy had felt as out of place at his house as he did at hers.

Savvy met him at the front door.

"Hi! Want to come in?" She stood aside and swept her arm toward a terrazzo foyer that covered more square footage than his whole house. Sunlight on crystal drew his eye upward to where a massive chandelier hung near a second-floor balustrade. A uniformed housekeeper went back to her dusting after he caught her checking him out.

"No thanks. I'm on my way to the coast. Here's your scarf."

"Thanks." She stared at the vicinity of his neck, where his face mask dangled. "Are you going swimming?"

"Diving."

Her eyebrows shot up, remembering.

"Want to come?" *¡Tonto del culo!* What was he thinking, inviting her along?

"Me?" Her hand pressed between her breasts, emphasizing their modest size and shape. She was wearing a black (of course) dress, but not a fancy one today. More like a long T-shirt with a V-neck.

"I-I couldn't. I can't. I have—" She floundered with her hands, seemingly at a loss.

His face must have revealed his disappointment.

"Actually, yes! I have nothing better to do. I mean, that didn't come out right. I don't know. . . . Were you serious?"

"If I didn't mean it, I wouldn't have asked. C'mon." He took a step toward the truck. "Let's go."

"I can't simply run out the door and go diving with you, without a plan! I don't know where it is, or how long we'll be gone, or what to wear or anything. . . ."

"Suit yourself." He threw up his hands and started across the porch. "Later . . ."

"Wait!" She bit her lip anxiously. "What do I need?"

"I have everything."

"When will we be back?"

He shrugged. "Depends."

"On what?"

¡Mierda! "How fast I catch my limit." He took another step toward the truck and waved her off. "You don't want to. It's okay. I'll see you next Wednes—"

"Wait right here! I'm coming. Let me grab my bag."

Esteban paced the broad porch. What had he got himself into? It was a two-hour drive to the coast. He'd be stuck with her for four hours in the Chevy, plus however much time they spent at the park.

At the same time, a jagged thrill tore through him. Four hours of staring at her legs on his truck seat. After they picked up Shane, she'd have to slide over next to him, almost touching his thigh with hers. He'd be able to smell her sweet scent. Feel the warmth coming off her body.

She reappeared with her purse and they were off.

"Where are we going?" she asked, clicking on her seat belt.

"Salt Point State Park."

"How long does it take to get there?"

"About two hours."

"What are we going to do, once we get there?"

"Park the truck, sit on the sand, and hopefully, find some abs."

Her eyes flew open as her hand pressed her chest again. "Me, get in the water?"

He grinned. "You bring your wet suit?"

"You said I didn't need anything," she frowned.

"*You* aren't getting in. That ocean water's about fifty-five degrees. Without a wet suit, you'd freeze to death. You don't know what do to, and besides, you need a license."

"So what am I going to do, then? Watch you from the beach?"

"That, and talk, apparently."

She swatted him.

"You want me to turn around?"

"No."

"There's a little strip of white sand in a protected cove."

A mile or so on, she finally relaxed enough to look around the truck's interior. "Where's all your stuff?"

He tossed his head toward the rear window. "Under the tarp."

"I should've brought a couple bottles of water for us. What about food? Two hours is a long time. There might not be many choices at the park and—"

"Do you always worry so much? Ask so many questions?"

She looked chagrinned, but the incessant questioning ceased, at least for the time being. It probably came with being a lawyer—having to know every detail of everything that was happening, before it happened. Must be hell. He felt a twinge of pity for her and her buttoned-up life.

"You're right about food. We'll stop before we get there."

"When?"

"Pretty soon."

"Where?"

He sighed and propped a wrist on the steering wheel, resigned. "Dry Creek General."

She smiled. "I like that store."

Gracias a Dios.

"The smell of curing meat and pepper from all those sausages hanging from the ceiling is a bit overwhelming, but it's a good smell."

She had that right. His mouth began to water just thinking about it.

He pulled off 101 into an unpaved lot. Inside, the old wood-paneled building was packed to the rafters with high-quality wine country merchandise, from knee-high baskets of gourmet chips, to glass jars of jerky, to tin vases stuffed with dogwood and morning glories. They got in line for sandwiches behind some pickers in work boots and a tourist lady with a brown handbag stamped in gold.

After Savvy ordered, Esteban put in his order for two sandwiches.

"A guy as big as you must have an appetite to match."

"The other one's for Shane."

"Shane?"

"We're picking him up along the way."

"We're taking someone else along?"

"Can't go ab diving alone."

"You didn't *tell* me that we'd have company."

He shrugged. "You didn't ask."

"I didn't know I had to ask that particular question! I might not have come if I'd known. . . ." Esteban let his eyes travel over the myriad sights of the store, grateful for something to look at while she prattled on.

Chapter 14

Savvy steamed. How dare Esteban haul her a hundred miles from her home without mentioning someone else was coming along! She never did anything unless it had been planned out to the nth degree. Flying by the seat of your pants wasn't what got you into Boston University School of Law, and it sure wasn't how you kept up your average, once you got there. Hopping blithely into his truck on the spur of the moment had been a big mistake.

While they waited in the long line of people to pay, Savvy tried to decide who was the best candidate to ask for a lift back to Napa.

That's when she noticed that every woman in the place—and some of the men—had their eyes peeled on Esteban, every chance they got. What was it about him, apart from his size and his obvious good looks? Something solid and authentic. Like Dry Creek General itself, there was nothing phony about him.

"Mind if I ask you a question?"

"You just did."

"Which side of the family did you get your height from?"

He lit up. She must have finally hit on something he liked talking about.

"My grandfather Morales. There's an old family legend. Ever hear of the Patagonian Indian tribe, from South America? Magellan called them giants. They were the first people he saw when his ship landed there, five hundred years ago. He claimed he and his men only came up to the Patagonian's waists."

"You're a Patagonian?"

He shrugged. "That's what my grandfather told me, when I asked him if I'd grow up to be as tall as he was." He grinned. "I'm still playing catchup to him and Uncle Esteban. They were both six-six."

They packed the cooler with ice and food and took off again, breeze blowing across them through the open windows.

When Esteban pulled up to a house in a neighborhood off Route 1, there was already a guy standing outside, waiting. Esteban got out to help him load his equipment into the truck bed.

The stranger opened the passenger-side door. "Shimmy over, sweet lips."

Before Savvy could take offense, he was jamming a soft-sided cooler into the space behind the seat.

Esteban slid in and made the introductions.

If anyone had told her she'd be spending her Sunday squeezed between two men on her way to who-knows-where, she'd have said he was crazy. Yet here she was, yanking down on the hem of her dress, each of her shoulders mere inches from one of theirs.

Grinning salaciously, Shane bent forward to address Esteban, as if she were deaf. "Where ya been hidin' her?"

She felt Esteban's shoulder stiffen. When he ignored the question, Shane turned his attention to her.

"You like abs?"

Savvy forced a tight smile. She was stuck here, and they still had miles to go. Maybe she should overlook Shane's comment, give him the benefit of the doubt. He might just be simple-minded. Ignorant, yet nothing to be afraid of. After all, he was Esteban's friend, wasn't he? Esteban wouldn't put her in danger. Somehow, she knew that.

"I've only tasted them once. Yes. They're good."

Shane's eyes flicked to her bare knees, and she squeezed them together involuntarily.

The men talked fishing while Savvy focused on staring straight out the windshield and not letting any of her body parts touch theirs. Before long, the road curved to the right to hug the Sonoma Coast, and watching for the sporadic views of the cliffs and the Pacific far below Route 1 absorbed everyone's attention.

"Almost there," said Esteban.

Shane slid his arm around her. She flinched until she realized he was only digging in his cooler behind the seat. When he pulled out a beer and popped the top, she said, "You can't drink that in here."

Shane took a swig. "Watch me." He grinned defiantly.

"I can't be in a car with an open container. I'm a lawyer. If we get pulled over, I could be disbarred."

"Why're *you* gonna get disbarred, when I'm the one drinking?"

"It's the law. Everyone in the car is liable for arrest."

"Ah, quit worrying. Esteban's a good driver, aren't you, E? We're not gonna get stopped."

"I'm serious. Can't you just wait till we get there?"

"Can't you just relax?"

Savvy looked to Esteban. His eyes stayed glued to the road, his mouth a thin line. Eyes forward again, she assessed her situation, tamping down her rising hysteria. She hated being at the mercy of other people. Trapped next to an idiot in a speeding vehicle, not knowing precisely where she was, where she was going, she might as well be hurtling off a cliff.

Mentally, she tried to talk herself down. Maybe she *was* overly anxious. Esteban wasn't drinking. That was the important thing. Besides, he'd said they were almost there.

Shane chugged his beer, tossed it onto the floor of the cab, and reached around her again.

She shot him an incredulous look. "Another one?" Quick as a wink, she bent down, picked up the empty and tossed it out the window on Esteban's side.

"Hey! Who's worse, me for drinking a beer or you for trashing the countryside?"

"Better to trash the environment than my career, or have Esteban suspected of DUI. Don't you know anything? If we get stopped with that can on the floor, it's probable cause to investigate the driver for drinking. It's one thing to put yourself in jeopardy, and you don't know me from Adam, but you ought to give a care about your friend."

"We're here," said Esteban coolly, pulling off the freeway onto an unpaved road.

Beer wedged between his knees, Shane reached inside his jacket, pulled out a blunt, and lit it.

"That's it! Stop the damn car!" yelled Savvy.

"E, control your bitch," said Shane mildly.

Esteban braked hard. Savvy's hand flew to the dashboard. Shane's beer sloshed out the hole in the top of the can.

"Get out," Esteban growled.

Wagging his head, Shane stuck the joint between his smiling lips, freeing up his beer-wet hands to gather his gear.

With the truck idling in the middle of the park's entrance, Esteban hopped out to turn back the tarp. Savvy heard shuffling and saw something fly by in the rearview mirror—probably part of Shane's stuff.

"Find your own way back," Savvy heard Esteban say above the engine.

"Fuck you," Shane replied, blowing smoke in the window at Savvy. He raised his middle finger high as he sauntered off toward the Pacific.

Esteban got back in and shifted into drive.

"And fuck your tight-ass girlfriend, too," Shane hollered as they passed him in a cloud of dust.

With a glance out the rear window, she said, "That jerk's your *friend*?"

"*Was.*"

"How do you know him?"

"I went to school with his cousin, Hector. He brought him along to dive a couple of times. Hector's actually pretty cool. Shane must be the dick in the family. Every family has one. You know how it is."

How true.

"Think I heard Hector's in the wine business now."

Savvy rolled her eyes. "Who isn't?"

"Distribution or something."

She looked back again. "How's he going to get home?"

"Not my problem. There'll be others here. After last winter, today's conditions'll bring out the divers from all over."

The dirt road ended before a sandy cove. Sure enough, a half dozen other vehicles sat askew in the clearing. Off the coast, waves broke over hundreds of rugged rocks.

Savvy followed Esteban around to the truck bed. He handed her what looked like an inflated red canvas pillow.

"Here. I'll carry the cooler, and you can carry my dive float."

"You're still going to dive—without a buddy?" Her anxiety returned. "Is that safe? What happens if you get in troub—"

"There's an inner tube inside the float. Gives me something to hang on to when I come up for air. I'm not going out as deep as I'd planned. Should be some good abs in the shallow areas. Today's opening day. They're not picked over yet."

They set out on a narrow trail leading to the north side of the cove, Esteban with the bulkier gear draped across his body, Savvy following with his float, through some tall bushes to a fork, where he turned down a ravine. Good thing she was behind him; once they got out of the trees, the wind whipped her dress up again and again until finally, she tied a knot in the hem, even though that shortened it to mid-thigh. Better that than swirling around her waist. Near the water's edge, Esteban stopped at a small patch of sheltered white sand and spread two thin beach towels side by side.

Savvy peered around, shielding her eyes from the bright sunlight. She probably should've brought a sweatshirt. The sky was cloudless, but sixty-eight degrees felt different on the exposed coast from how it did in the valley. Behind them was a steep sea cliff. Though you couldn't see it from down here, she knew the freeway ran along its rim. Rocks in an infinite variety of forms and shapes dotted the spectacular sea vista. Farther north, the grassy hills were dotted with stunted cypress trees, tortured into weird shapes by the ceaseless winds.

He would be all right, she told herself. He had common sense. His size and strength made him seem invincible.

So he was going to dive alone. Not entirely, though. Savvy would be there, watching him from afar.

Chapter 15

"This is my buoy. One end's attached to my anchor—see? It screws into the sandy bottom—and my flag's on the other. That way everyone can tell at a glance there's a diver down below." Esteban held up the end of a flexible black belt lined with pouches, its heft obvious from the way it hung. "My weight belt. The pockets are filled with lead shot, like sandbags. That compensates for the positive buoyancy created by my wet suit."

The clear explanations given in his confident tone of voice had a calming effect on Savvy. He sounded like he knew what he was doing. Reluctant to seem like even more of a nervous Nellie, she bit her tongue.

Her face must've given her away. He added, "I've been doing this since I was a kid."

"A little kid? You mean, like a ten-year-old? Or a teenager? Don't you have to be a certain age—?"

He stopped her with a halting hand. "Trust me, Savvy. A kid."

Her name on his lips replaced her anxiety with that melty feeling. For some reason, she did trust Esteban. Wasn't he the boy next door? She'd sat in his dining chair. She knew his *mami*, for God's sake. Plus, if anything happened to him, she'd kill him.

Esteban dropped his weight belt, propped his hands on his hips, and looked out to sea.

"See the floats and the dive flags out there?"

She could barely make out the red squares with the diagonal white lines, bobbing to the south.

Nonchalantly, he pulled off his T-shirt and tossed it onto a towel, catching Savvy totally by surprise. She averted her eyes from the rippling contours of his torso. But when he stepped out of his Levi's, her eyes got a mind of their own, fastening themselves to his narrow hips, his long shanks.

Heaven help her. Was that even legal? A truck farmer in a Speedo?

He lay back on his towel and propped himself up on his elbows, a delicious stretch of caramel-colored man-god.

"You want to watch the ocean a while, before you dive. Scope out the biggest wave you're likely to encounter, get the pattern of the wave sets," he said over the crashing of the water and the wind.

Somehow, Savvy managed to un-drop her jaw. What the heck was she supposed to do now? Stand there like some—what was it Shane had called her? Tight-ass?

Kicking off her sandals, she lowered herself to the other towel, aping his position. She stole a glance at his splayed legs. Her natural tendency was to cross hers at the ankles . . . but apparently, not his. Then again, he had a certain . . . *impediment* that she lacked. In fact, maybe crossing his legs wasn't even a possibility. The thought boggled the mind.

With difficulty, she tore her gaze off his lower half to watch a pelican dive into the spray, then let her head drop back to follow an osprey riding a wind current. She could do this.

She pointed to some flat, bronze-colored formations on the shore. "What are those honeycomb patterns in the rocks?"

"Those are tafoni. Caused by the constant pounding of the salt water. The composition of the sandstone is tight in some places, loose in others. That's what makes that lacy pattern."

Savvy nodded.

Long, dark strands of his hair blew back, exposing his profile. "This sun feels great," he said. He lay back again with his hands behind his head and closed his eyes.

Savvy gulped. His face in repose was beautiful, his roped biceps pure, male muscle. Some men lifted barbells, others shoveled compost, she supposed.

She studied the smooth planes and valleys of his torso. She recalled hearing somewhere that North American Indians didn't have much body hair. She wondered what—

Whoa!

Unexpectedly, Esteban turned on his side, his entire . . . er, *package* . . . flopping over with him.

Might CVS let her return those size-medium condoms in her collection?

His forearm skimmed her stomach when he reached across her for the cooler, sending a shockwave through her.

Must. Act. Normal. As if lying beside a naked copy of the David in public was something she did on a regular basis. She couldn't show the way she really felt, like Jell-O inside, all wet and wobbly.

"So, what do you think? How's it look out there?" she asked, faking a world-weary yawn.

"Awesome." He tilted back his Coke bottle and gulped half of it down.

So why wasn't he splashing into the waves this very minute, instead of lying here on the sand next to her? That's what achievement-oriented Savvy would be doing, instead of—

"Doesn't look too bad right here, either," he said in answer to her unspoken thought, eyeing her lazily.

For once, Savvy was tongue-tied. Her hands chafed to touch him. She couldn't remember the last time she'd simply sat still and enjoyed the scenery. She was always working toward something. Grades, the bar exam, a promotion. Her gelatinous insides and pounding pulse only added to her confusion.

He rolled over onto his stomach, his face inches from hers. "Sorry about that thing with Shane. He's not worth getting riled up over." He fingered the ribbed edging of her sleeve, making the skin on her upper arm tingle where the backs of his fingers brushed against it.

Shane? What Shane?

"If I weren't worried about losing my license to practice, maybe I wouldn't have freaked so badly . . ." she managed to get out.

"I can't believe he lit up a doobie with you in my truck." He grinned with the memory.

"Is that what you two do when you're together?"

"Smoke weed?" He—and his Patagonian package—rolled back over with a chuckle. "Never tried the stuff. I've only been around Shane a few times, diving."

Something about the water caught his eye.

"Speaking of which, I think it's time. Surf's low, tide's high."

He got up and pulled a black wet suit from his duffel. Savvy couldn't tear her eyes away from his upper arms, thighs, and calves as they contracted and relaxed in his struggle to wedge himself into it. Now she saw the purpose of the Speedo. It'd be really hard to tuck board shorts into that skin-tight neoprene that molded to his body.

"Will you be warm enough?"

"Never fun having ice-cold water streaming up your legs, but you get used to it."

He stuck a wicked-looking knife into a sheath on his weight belt as a finishing touch.

"What do you consider shallow?"

"Fifteen feet or so, where the reef begins. You'll see my flag." He fiddled with the strap on his face mask, propping it up on his head until he needed it, then slung his red float onto his back and set out for the waterline.

"You look like a giant turtle that's walking upright," she said.

Without turning around, he raised a hand to acknowledge he'd heard her. "That's what everyone says the first time they see abalone divers."

"How long can you hold your breath?" she called after him.

"Long enough," he shouted back.

"Don't worry about me. I'll be waiting," she yelled. *Right here. By myself. Worrying.*

He stopped in his tracks, paused, then turned and marched back to her until his face was mere inches from hers.

"Let's get one thing straight," he said, dead serious. "Don't get in the water. No matter what. You know that, right?"

She nodded once. "Right."

He turned and started back.

She couldn't control herself. "What if something happens to you?"

He stopped again, his shoulders rising and falling in resignation before he turned and trudged back to her yet again.

"Nothing's going to happen, but if it does, scream and wave your arms to those guys out there."

"M'kay," she said in a small voice to his back.

Chapter 16

Esteban knew better than to dive alone. But he'd driven all the way out here, and it was his first dive after that endless winter. This might be the only time he'd get out in the foreseeable future. Next to tending his precious lavender plants, whose progress wasn't exactly encouraging, diving was his favorite pastime. The only thing he spent his hard-earned extra money on was on dive gear. His wet suit alone had set him back five hundred bucks. He'd like to get his money's worth.

Plus, he had Savvy with him, and his macho blood wouldn't let him look like a *verga* in front of her.

He'd be fine.

He set a game plan. Fifteen dives, one minute each, and done. If he could lie on the sand with Savvy awhile, steal a few kisses, and eat a dinner of subs and fresh abalone, he'd go to bed happy tonight.

He always winced at that moment when the icy water seeped into his suit, but today was different. Today Esteban felt Savvy's cola-colored eyes burning a hole through him. He couldn't let his body language show weakness. Uttering a choice Spanish oath, he forced himself to walk without hesitation into the roiling surf.

Once the water reached his spine, he knew it wouldn't get any worse. When he got to the rocks, he lowered his mask, bit into his snorkel, and peered under the water to check on the kelp situation. It was too early in the year for seaweed to be visible above the water-line, but he knew the slippery stuff had already begun growing down there, attaching itself to the rocks, providing a home for all sorts of marine life—including abalone.

A quick glance didn't turn up much. Hardly any kelp at all in this location, but the visibility was only one to two feet due to the turbulence. He'd have to go out a little farther.

He came up and squinted across the sparkly water at Savvy lounging on the beach, blissfully ignorant. He'd let her believe what most non-divers thought—that shallow diving was safer than deep. Truth was, going down below fifteen feet was actually both easier and safer. At that depth, the waves were just gentle swells. Up here, it was hard to see, and the rough waves wore out a diver a lot faster.

There was another reason he didn't want to go out too far, too. He wanted to keep an eye on her.

He looked around. A stretch of reef forty feet farther out looked vaguely familiar. If that was the spot he thought it was, he'd taken a few nice-size abs from it a couple years back. He started swimming, towing his float with his gear on top of it.

The closer he got, the more he liked what he saw. There was a nice stretch of rock wall down there, with lots of promising holes where abs loved to hide.

After setting his flag and anchoring his buoy, he adjusted the weight on his belt until he reached neutral buoyancy.

Next, he floated on his back for a minute, breathing deeply to build up oxygen in his blood. *Dios,* it was cold. When he was ready, he blew the water out of his snorkel, reached down with one arm, and lifted the opposite leg straight into the air in a smooth motion, letting his body weight propel him down, down until his feet entered the water and he could further drive himself by kicking.

Under the water, he righted himself and relaxed. This *was* the reef he'd fished before. He thought about presenting a big fat abalone to Savvy . . . savoring its fresh taste with her.

Neon-bright anemones swayed in the frigid green water. A couple of starfish drifted along the bottom, at the whim of the currents. A shy greenling hurried away from him with a flick of his tail. Farther away, some coral caught his eye. These first few dives were only for recon. Once he spotted an ab that looked like it met the seven-inch requirement, he'd gauge it to check. Sometimes they appeared bigger through the mask than they actually were. If it was a good one, he'd try to pry it off the reef before it saw him and clamped onto the rock. You had to work fast so you didn't startle the ab or run out of breath, and he felt like a thief every time, measuring as fast as he could, sliding his pry knife between the snail and the rock, the whole job over in a matter of seconds.

He spotted a clutch of ribbed fan shells—scallops—and bent to scoop them up as a nice addition to their supper, but an unexpected wave rolled in and swept him away from the reef, scattering the scallops with it. With a hard scissor kick, he righted himself and climbed up . . . up. Breaking the surface, he sucked air into his lungs and shook his hair out of his eyes. He was farther from his float than he'd thought. Getting back to it would use up precious extra energy.

He went back and looked for the scallops, but they were gone, dispersed by the chop. So he flashed his light under the rocky outcroppings where the big boys liked to hide, careful not to give himself away by swirling the water. No luck.

The water made his bones ache. Fifteen dives might be pushing it. He had to find something in, maybe, ten.

On his fourth dive he spotted some abs, none of them legal. At least he knew he was in the right place. There was a nice horizontal opening he wanted to check out next.

He reached his glove into the crevice and sure enough, felt a big, flattened football shape. Quick as a wink, he rammed his pry bar under it and *bam,* pulled out a nice, heavy ab. *Yes!* He couldn't wait to show Savvy. Kicking with all his might, he swam toward the light, broke the surface, and held it up. Her return wave compensated a little for his shivering. He slipped it into a pocket in his float, sucked in some more air, and headed back down.

One ab down, two to go for his daily legal limit of three. It'd be great if he could find one for Madre, too. She loved abs almost as much as—

Esteban's mind went blank as a rogue force sucked his head down into the water, then dragged his body back with it. His snorkel was ripped from his mouth. Everything went white and bubbly. Where was he? Which way was up? Over and over he tumbled until his back banged up against the sharp reef. *Mierda. That hurt.*

When he finally clawed to the surface, lungs screaming for air, he spun left, then right. *Where was his float?* He caught a couple flashes of crimson way off to—was that south? Confusion clouded his brain. No. Those flags belonged to the divers he and Savvy had seen earlier. And then he saw his own beautiful float, rising and falling in the waves a good sixty feet back toward the shore.

I'm done. He panted, treading water until he caught enough breath to swim. He attempted to fix his snorkel, but his fingers were too clumsy. It took several tries before he finally got it twisted around under his mask strap and into his mouth. He'd just get back to the float and call it a day. He was lucky it'd been his back that bashed against the rocks and not his head.

By the time he reached base, he realized he wasn't shivering any more. Now he felt strangely calm. Almost . . . drowsy. He blinked and shook his head. He couldn't give up yet. He needed one more ab. One for Savvy, one for . . . who was it that he wanted it for again? He'd remember later. Right now, he had to go down one last time. . . .

Savvy was on her feet, looking out to sea. She hadn't seen Esteban in—three minutes? Four?

She'd been staring at the same spot for so long she was beginning to imagine things that weren't there. Still, she couldn't tear her gaze away from that red flag, its carefree bobbing against the bright blue sky making a mockery of her fear.

When she thought she spotted his head in the trough of a wavelet on the far side of his float, she stood on her toes and craned her neck. *Please, be him. What is he doing all the way out there, the stupid—tsk.*

"Please, come in now," she whispered. But he couldn't hear her. No one could. She was helpless and completely, utterly alone.

Her mind swam with all the things they'd done wrong. He shouldn't have dived by himself. She shouldn't have let him. She hadn't even thought to check his departure time on her phone. How long had he been out there? Probably no longer than twenty-five minutes, though it seemed like hours. She'd stuck a toe in the surf a while ago, only to jump back in shock. How could anyone withstand being completely immersed in that temperature? And for such a long time?

Exasperated, she huffed and looked around yet again for someone, anyone, to call on. But the divers Esteban had shown her had moved farther down the coast. Shane might still be back by the cars. By the time she ran *there,* though, Esteban might be back *here,* needing her. Not that she had a clue how to help him, or even the kind of trouble he might run into. What were the ways he'd said divers got hurt, back when they were sitting at the bar at Bodega? Riptides? Exhaustion? Getting stuck in a hole?

Where is he? She focused on the flag, willing him to appear, while the minutes ticked by.

Finally she let her aching arm fall from where her hand had shaded her eyes for so long, and paced the sand, only to stop and peer out again. How far was it to the float? How deep? How long would it take her to wade and swim out there? Could she make it without hurting herself, making things worse? And what about her glasses? She couldn't see a thing without them.

Where are you, Esteban? Maybe that was his head, bobbing among those of the other divers down the coast. No. He never could have made it that far. She was grasping at straws.

She cupped her mouth. "Esteban!" she screamed, knowing in her heart of hearts it was useless.

Desperately, she looked around for something, anything useful. Grabbing a towel, she turned toward the other cluster of divers, their flags tiny postage stamps flapping in the wind, and jumped up and down, waving it back and forth. "Hey! Help!"

The seagulls laughed and laughed.

Her phone. She snatched it, punched in 911, and waited. No service. They were too far out. In disgust, she flung it onto Esteban's pile of clothes.

She'd taken a lifesaving class when she was thirteen. Everyone had to take it back at Five Oaks. It was required—and why was she even thinking about middle school now when she should be out there, finding him?

She whipped off her dress—*you were right about the frumpy skivvies, Mer, ugh*—folded her glasses, jammed them in her bag, and ran down the beach and splashed into the water, the sharp rocks crucifying her feet. She'd get off them and start swimming as soon as—*Ahhhhhhggg!* It was freaking freezing!

"Esteban!" she screamed as her chest hit the surf. Then she remembered. He had a wet suit. She had nothing. But now she was committed.

"Esteban!" Her voice was consumed by the roar of the wind and the crash of the tide. She struggled to stay on the surface of the cold, turbulent sea. A wave washed over her and she choked on a mouthful of salt water. Long strands of hair pulled loose from her chignon, whipping in her face, blocking her already useless eyesight.

The float was a vague red shape in a world of green and white. If she could only keep her eye on it, she could reach it, hang on to it, and decide what to do from there. The current rushed by perpendicular to her as she fought to keep going.

Bizarre thoughts rushed through her head, like that time her car had hydroplaned and it was flying diagonally across the dotted white line, out of control, and she was in a time warp, completely powerless waiting for it to crash over the opposite bank, even though she knew that in the next few seconds there was going to be major hell to pay in terms of a permanently scarred face or broken limbs or at the very least, big-time vehicular damage. She might die of hypothermia before she ever reached that damn float . . . or get eaten by a shark. Esteban was going to be pissed. . . . This was going to ruin her plans to seduce him. . . . She'd spent all that time picking out that new green dress—why green? She never wore green—and that lacy white underwear for nothing. If only her arms could move as fast as her brain, because she didn't care if she never made that land deal, never made partner, none of that mattered now. All that mattered was getting to Esteban. Saving him.

It was taking forever.

"Esteban!"

And then she imagined she glimpsed a black hood. Was that him, hanging off the side of the float? If he could see her splashing toward him, why wasn't he waving back? Yelling at her for disobeying him? Saying hello, good-bye, or go to hell?

She dug down deep, mustering the reserves to up her pace, cycling her arms, keeping her head out of the water, her eye on the blurry prize. She'd never swum so fast or so hard, or been so cold.

And the whole time she swam, she had a terrible dread that something was very, very wrong. At long last, she flung herself onto the float. "Esteban!"

"S-Savvy?"

"Esteban! What's wrong with you?" she gasped. "Where were you? Didn't you see me coming? Why didn't you answer me?"

"C-c-cold," he stuttered. "S-s-sleepy."

She gaped at him in disbelief, shoving the wet hair out of her eyes with numb fingers. *Cold? Damn right it was cold! Bracing, not sedating. He sure picked a helluva time to take a nap. . . .*

A line from that middle-school water safety class came back to her.

The main symptoms of hypothermia are confusion, slurred speech, and drowsiness.

"Esteban, listen to me. Hold on to the float. I'm going to get us back." She grabbed onto a nylon rope and took a stroke in the direction of the shore, only getting a short distance before she felt an opposing tug. *It's anchored. To the bottom.* She couldn't waste precious time, breath, and energy diving down who-knew-how-deep to figure out how to undo it. Besides, she wouldn't be able to see down there.

"Esteban. Hand me your knife."

Behind his mask, his eyelids fluttered.

"Esteban!" She slapped the side of his head. "Give me your knife! I need it, now!"

His head fell back. At least he'd had the presence of mind to loop a rope attached to the float through a carabiner on the shoulder of his wet suit before he lost consciousness.

"Wake up!" Her hands blazed a trail down his firm body. His fingers were fumbling around his waistline, too, getting in her way.

"Move your hands!" she screamed, shoving at them in frustration. What was he doing, making this harder?

"Bell," Esteban mumbled.

Bell? What bell?

"Belt."

That's right—his belt is weighted!

Seemingly in slow motion, her unfeeling fingers combed through the viscous water, found the plastic buckle, and at last felt it unclick. Victory! The heavy belt slipped away, and Esteban's body floated upward. Seeing the knife strapped to his thigh, she ripped open the snap securing it and withdrew it from its sheath.

Next, she reached under the float, holding the line taut with one hand, slicing with the other. One pass of the knife, and the float sprang free.

The problem now was, did she have the strength to pull them both back through the perpendicular current?

In case of riptide, don't fight the current. Swim parallel to the shore until you come out of it.

Thank you, water safety manual. Thank you, Five Oaks, and my annoyingly compulsive need to excel at every class I ever took, even lifesaving. Especially *lifesaving.*

Chapter 17

Something lay along Esteban's chest. Something warm and firm, yet pliable, like the big old hound he used to sneak into his bed when he was six years old that Madre would shoo back out to the porch after Esteban had fallen asleep.

"Esteban?" A female voice broke through the veil of his subconscious.

Esteban?

What was that roar? The sea. The wind. Oh yeah. They were at the coast. He'd know that sound anywhere.

"You're all right. You're going to be okay. Oh, thank you, God, thank you," the voice cried.

The warm weight rolled off of him. "Help!" he heard a holler. "Somebody help us!"

And then the presence was back, stroking his cheek, murmuring assurances again and again. A thin covering was being pulled up to his chin and tucked around his leaden body.

He coughed and it tasted like salt water.

"Are you awake?"

Through his squint, he saw the anxious face of a bedraggled mermaid hovering inches above his own.

Had he died? Was this some sort of abalone diver's heaven?

He blinked the facial features into hazy focus.

The mermaid smiled, the sun forming a halo behind her, bringing to mind an old church hymn. *Break forth O beauteous heav'nly light, and usher in the morning . . .*

"Your teeth are really white."

Her laugh rang with relief. "So are yours."

"¿*Qué pasa?* Are you an angel?"

"You got too cold out there. I think you have hypothermia."

He tried to think, but it was taking a while to get his head in gear. "How'd I get in?"

"I brought you."

He hefted his weight up onto an elbow. "You?" A more beautiful face than hers he'd never seen. He blinked again, eyes flickering further down. For a mermaid, she sure wore an ugly bra. And he'd never known mermaids wore glasses.

He fell back coughing, putting a hand to his forehead. It was starting to come back to him now. Fighting the arctic waves, tiring, knowing he should go in, but too stubborn.

He'd felt himself slipping, slipping away into a frigid, eternal darkness.

His head lolled to his left to gaze at the vision kneeling over him on the sand, skeins of wet auburn hair plastered to slender shoulders. He removed her glasses and set them aside, then curled his hand around the back of her head, brought it down, and kissed her, seeking her warmth. Craving her vital force. She unfolded herself to lie back down and press herself against him again, snaking her arms around his neck.

As he sucked on her lower lip, then savored the textures of her mouth, it all came rushing back to him, moment by treacherous moment.

I'm alive.

The stark reality of what could have been tempered all other thoughts, principles, and rules of conduct.

He kissed her until he ran out of breath. And then he kissed her some more, devouring her like the dying man he'd narrowly escaped becoming. As if she were life itself.

He had to have her—all of her—right there on that beach, under that blazing blue sky. It wasn't an idea or a choice. It was a mandate. Nothing else mattered. Greedily, his hands molded her flesh. No sooner did he discover one delicious curve than he had to tear himself away to capture another, and then another.

Their clothes were gone.

He didn't know how. It didn't matter. Coercion played no part in this. Morality, either. She returned his advances with an eagerness that matched his own. They were two primordial creatures, at one with the earth, sea, and sky, their cries of righteous satisfaction swirling into the atmosphere on the unceasing wind.

When it was over, she collapsed onto his chest. He held her there until the rhythmic rise and fall of her breathing slowed, finger-combing her tangled locks into the hollow between her shoulder blades.

"Ahhhhhhhh," she sighed into his shoulder.

Cradling her head in his hands, he raised it and peered up into her naked eyes, so pretty without those glasses. Emotion swelled his heart. "Are you good?"

She smiled lazily. "You have no idea." With her leading, they rolled onto their sides, facing each other.

"Me too."

"We're naked," she giggled.

He wouldn't have cared about his own skin even if he *didn't* feel newly invincible. Then again, he didn't want anyone else seeing *her* that way. He lifted his hips, whipping his towel out from under him so he could cover her up. That's when he saw the red blotch about two-thirds of the way down.

"Whose blood is that?" In a flash, he was sitting up, concerned eyes skimming her from head to toe. "Are you hurt somewhere? Did you get hurt on the rocks?"

She lay still, waiting for his eyes to complete their circuit of her body and return to hers.

She opened her lips as if to speak, then apparently changed her mind.

"No. Don't tell me. You're not—you weren't—"

Her silence was his answer.

"Savvy," he whispered. "Oh, Savvy." His throat filled with salt water again, but this time it wasn't from the ocean. He was over-whelmed with a rush of possessiveness. "You're mine now. You hear me?" He crushed her to his chest and rocked her while the seagulls screamed and the surf pounded against the shore.

All Esteban had ever cared about was getting up with the sun each morning, tending his little patch of ground, and hiking and diving when he could get away. Love—the romantic kind—was just something on the radio used to sell songs. Now, on a windswept beach, love had found him in the guise of a bespectacled mermaid, grabbed him by the throat, and shaken him senseless.

*   *   *

Meri gave Savvy a slanted glance when she caught her sashaying down the upstairs hallway to her room, well after dusk.

Savvy smiled a Mona Lisa smile.

Meri's hand flew to her mouth. "Oh. My. God. You did it."

Who cared who knew? Savvy was a completely new person now. A whole woman. Her blood flowed more powerfully through her veins than when she'd gotten up that morning. She held her head higher, walked taller, every step a reminder of the soreness in her most private place that served as proof.

"What?" Char's head popped out from her doorway.

"Savvy did the nae nae," Meri announced matter-of-factly.

Char made a face at Meri, then turned to Savvy. "Hey, Savv. What's going on?"

Savvy had cleaned up the best she could under the circumstances. Smoothed down her dress, twisted up her hair and fixed her makeup. Count on her sisters not to miss a trick.

"Where've you been? It's not like you to disappear all day."

"Out," she breathed, feeling regal as a queen.

"Out," aped Meri with a dramatic flip of her hair. "C'mon, spill it."

They tailed her into her room, first Meri, then Char, closing the door behind her.

"Is it him?" asked Meri. "Is it Esteban?"

Savvy huffed in mock disgust. "Can't a girl get any privacy around here?"

"Don't play coy. All three of us were dying to move back in together after all that time apart, and you know it."

Meri was right. Savvy flopped back on her duvet, spread eagle. "I'm in love," she sighed to the ceiling.

"Savvy! That's wonderful!" said Char.

"In love with the boy next door," Meri said. "Wait till Papa gets a load of this."

Savvy smiled dreamily.

"I'm so happy for you," said Char, lowering herself gracefully onto the bed. "You know who else will be thrilled? Jeanne. She's always been a fan of that family."

"Details, we want details." Meri hopped aboard, rocking everybody.

"I'm not ready. It's still raw," said Savvy, regretting her choice of words as soon as they were out.

"Please." Meri held up a hand. "Not that detailed."

Char patted Savvy's knee. "Let her be, Meri."

"Where were you? What's it like with a farmer boy? Pretty good, from the looks of you. You're a wreck."

"Meri! She said she's not ready."

"Just tell me one thing. You used protection, right?"

Savvy's smile disintegrated.

"Right?" Meri might be young, but she was wise in the ways of the world. There'd always been a certain *je ne sais quoi* about her.

Everything had happened so fast, so unexpectedly. "It was only once," said Savvy, subdued. "Besides, quote, 'any random act of intercourse only results in a pregnancy twenty percent of the time.' Unquote."

Meri pulled a face. "You looked up the stats?"

"Didn't have to. I aced Bio."

Anyway, it was too late for regrets now. She jumped up and headed for her bathroom. "Don't worry, I'll be fine. What I need is a nice, warm bubble bath. So, if you'll excuse me . . ."

Her phone rang and Esteban's name on the screen reignited her sultry grin.

"Hello?" she sang, waggling her fingers in a farewell to her sisters before closing the bathroom door on meddlesome eyes and ears.

"¡Ay!" Esteban winced as his mother put salve on the cut in the center of his back.

"This might sting."

"No kidding!"

"Hurt anywhere else?"

"No." *Everywhere.*

Savvy had just left the Morales house.

"Why did I have to wait two days to find out from Señorita Sauvignon that you scratched your back diving?" Madre scolded. "Why couldn't you tell me Sunday night, as soon as you got home?"

Because he wasn't a wuss, and besides, Sunday night all he'd wanted to do was be alone with his thoughts, to savor the memory of making love to a mermaid.

"Very nice of her to bring you a present."

Savvy had stopped by after work tonight with a gift certificate to an online dive shop.

When he'd called her Monday afternoon, she'd assured him she was fine. No bumps or bruises from hauling his sorry ass out of the water. More importantly, no regrets over what had gone down afterward. He'd insisted on seeing for himself though, taking the Chevy over, climbing the steps to knock on the front door of Domaine St. Pierre after his day in the fields, despite his sore limbs and the stinging gash on his back. Leaving her with the best thank-you he knew: the abalone he'd salvaged, pounded thin, iced in a plastic bag.

"A fine lady, and generous, too, bringing you a present for nothing."

With an impatient tug, he started lowering his shirt. Madre had no idea that certificate was to be used toward the replacement of the belt and knife Savvy had let fall to the bottom of the ocean when she'd saved his life. And she never would. Not if he could help it.

"Not so fast, Señor. Let me put a bandage on that."

Impatiently, he leaned on the kitchen sink and waited while she sifted through a drawer. Madre didn't get to play nursemaid much anymore.

"I saw you kissing her at her car before she left."

He rolled his eyes. One of the downsides to living with your parents.

"I think she likes you, too. The way she threw her arms around your neck—"

"Okay. That's good." He whipped around, straightening to his full height.

"Be careful!" she scolded.

He tugged his shirt down. "We're done here."

"Esteban, wait." She laid a hand on his arm.

Now what?

"We have to talk. What you're going to do about Padre's counteroffer?"

Did she think that had slipped his mind? It was bad enough before he'd taken Savvy's virginity to know that he'd been less than completely truthful with her. Now, it was eating him up inside.

"Lying is never good."

"I know that, Mami, but it's not really a lie."

"Listen to me. It's easy. You just tell her what is Padre's offer."

True, Madre could talk anyone into buying cantaloupes and cabbages—in dual languages, no less. She was the best asset the family had when it came to peddling their produce. But the average total purchase down at the market was about twenty bucks. Anyone who could afford to make offers in the millions was a major wheeler dealer. Madre had no experience with the likes of them.

"Savvy's clients would laugh her out of town if she went back to them with that figure. Anyway, Padre meant it half as a joke. It's just his way of saying he won't sell, at any price."

Madre shrugged her shoulders. "So, they laugh? At least it will be over and done. No one will be able to accuse you of twisting their words."

She had a point. No one in his right mind would pay two million dollars for their boggy bottomland. And since he was certain that price *was* Padre's final word on the subject, all he had to lose was his pride. Better to be humiliated and have it off his chest.

"Not only that, you'll feel better inside." She patted his back, right on the sore spot.

"*¡Ay!*"

Chapter 18

Savvy smiled at Esteban as they strolled down the city sidewalk toward Smells Like Napa, the skirt of her springy green dress swirling around her legs as she walked.

Never had she felt so attractive. So alluring. *So sexy.* The unfamiliar crispness of new lace hugging the crease where her legs met her body only intensified the feeling. As it turned out, all that time and money spent on new underwear had been unnecessary. Everything had happened so fast that Sunday at the coast...all the drama and emotion of the near-tragedy channeled into a magical act of passion. A week and a half later, she still hadn't floated back to earth. By the set of his chin and the pride with which he carried himself, neither had Esteban. Arm linked through his, she tugged her god of agriculture closer to her side.

Those condoms would still come in handy, though—if they could ever find a little privacy. It was hard to be alone when you both lived with your parents, unless you wanted to go the super-obvious route and rent a hotel room or something. They'd figure something out. As soon as her caseload calmed down, she was planning on going shopping again, building a whole new underwear wardrobe, in all the colors of the rainbow. No more Ms. Beige.

When they got to the shop, Esteban held the door, and she gazed up at him adoringly. Inside, she pulled up short, closed her eyes, and inhaled, transported to a place of peace and romance by the all-encompassing aroma. She was glad she'd opted not to wear fragrance today so she could focus solely on the scents of grapes and olives and herbs.

She opened her eyes to shelves brimming with baskets, bottles, and boxes competing for her attention. Which direction to head first? Candles? Bath products? Soaps?

Barely visible behind the counter stacked high with dried bundles of lavender, a sales associate was in the midst of a dialog with a customer.

". . . and currently the best we have is one made by Welsh monks, but as you know, we like to keep it local whenever possible."

"When Lucas and I bought the ranch ten years ago, there was a built-in distillery there, but we've never even gone near it. Lucas had just retired from the tech industry and I was a clinical psychologist and professor. We had this idea that we wanted a little piece of land, maybe grow a few vegetables and herbs for our own use. Who knew lavender grew like wildfire in our rocky soil?" said the woman with the silver braid, whose back was toward Savvy.

"I'm going to go check out those lotions over there," Savvy whispered to Esteban, pointing. Casually, she meandered nearer the women and picked up a random bottle, pretending to scrutinize the writing on the back.

"Farming is harder than most folks realize," the clerk sympathized.

"Even if I did have the time and energy, there's a lot of expertise that goes into composing a commercially successful perfume. Aside from distilling the oil, the real trick is combining the base note with middle and top notes. It takes years of study. To be honest, I'm content to have your place to bring a few bundles of my lavender to. If nothing else, coming into town a few times a year fools me into believing I still have some semblance of a social life."

From their body language, they were saying their farewells, but Savvy didn't hear another word over the blood rushing in her ears. Out of the blue, she saw herself pouring potions back and forth between test tubes like some mad scientist. Blending, sniffing, creating. It wasn't like her, indulging in that kind of frivolity. She already had a job—one she wasn't doing too well at. Her cheeks warmed when she thought of her original plan to use sex as a tool to get to Esteban. That plan was all in the past now.

Excelling as a lawyer was a goal she couldn't afford to give up, though. It wasn't like she could rest on her laurels, put in her time. Witmer, Robinson and Scott had an "up or out" policy. Most law firms did. If you weren't productive enough to make partner within a certain number of years, you were politely asked to leave.

If she was fired, who would take care of Papa and her sisters? Papa had already had his share of run-ins with the law, and knowing him, there'd be more to come. Who would be there to bail him out? As for her more law-abiding sisters, who better than Savvy to write their prenups, keep an eye on their complicated personal estates? She still had nightmares about the times when they'd needed her and her hands were tied. *Never again.*

"May I help you?"

The clerk's voice startled Savvy out of her thoughts. "I hope so. The woman you were talking to. Do you mind if I ask her name?"

"You mean Anne Rathmell? She and her husband own a ranch on the county line. They grow the most amazing lavender. She came to drop off these bundles."

She handed Savvy an armful of the purple flowers bound up in raffia.

The stalks rustled in her hands. "They're gorgeous. I didn't mean to eavesdrop, but I couldn't help overhearing what you were saying about perfume-making."

"Oh, that." She lifted her chin. "I'm always on the lookout for an excellent-quality personal fragrance based on lavender."

"Is that so hard to find?"

"There are a few out there, but most of them are from Europe. Lavender's originally a Mediterranean plant, you know? Are you in the market for a fragrance?" She reached into a glass case and pulled out a box tied with a satin bow. "I get this when I travel to Wales. They won't ship it to the U.S. Here"—she picked up a sampler—"let me see your wrist."

"Just a little spritz. I'm highly sensitive to smells." Dutifully, she held out her forearm. As the woman was poised to spray, Savvy gasped. "That looks like my sister's bracelet!"

The woman tilted her head in surprise. "Your sister is Merlot St. Pierre, the jewelry designer?"

Savvy nodded enthusiastically. "That piece you're wearing is from her Entwined Collection."

"Yes, I know," said the woman, fingering the fine gold wire looping her wrist. "My interest in all things local extends to what I wear.

As soon as I saw this piece, though, I knew I had to have it. I would have bought it even if it hadn't been made by a famous Napan."

"You know, her line was just bought by Harrington's." Savvy couldn't help giving Meri a little plug.

"I do." Her smile held a twinge of regret. "I'd carry your sister's jewelry myself if Harrington's didn't have an exclusive." She extended her hand. "My name's Elizabeth Hull. I'm the owner here."

"I'm Savvy." She deflated a little. If Elizabeth knew of Domaine St. Pierre, that meant she'd also heard about the family scandals.

"Sauvignon. I recognize you now! How are you and your sisters adjusting, now that you're all back home in Napa?"

"Great! Fine."

She leaned in, lowering her voice. "Is Chardonnay still seeing that actor? Everyone's talking about it."

Despite its world renown, at its heart Napa was just another small town that loved its gossip.

"Um . . . can I try that fragrance?"

"Oh! Of course." Elizabeth sprayed, and Savvy cautiously inhaled. Her eyelids fluttered closed. "Tell me what words come to mind."

"Flowery. Honey. Herbal.' "

"*Angustifolia*, English lavender, sometimes called true lavender. Or French lavender, when it comes from France. Real French lavender, *dentate*, is an annual that comes from Spain. It's similar to English lavender in size, except the leaves are toothed."

Savvy put a hand to her forehead, and the clerk laughed.

"Confused? Don't feel bad, everyone is. Then there's Dutch lavender, *intermedia,* which has higher levels of camphor and other terpenes."

"Well, whatever it's called, this one's lovely. My—er, friend over there is trying to teach me about the different plant species and varieties. What I'm really interested in, though, is a locally sourced perfume."

The woman eyed Esteban up and down, then raised an eyebrow. "Between you and me, you have excellent taste in 'friends,' " she said. "Anyway, if you find a Cali product as good as this one, be sure to let me know. It'd be a runaway bestseller."

"Northern California's climate is similar to the Mediterranean's. Isn't a lot of lavender grown around here?"

"To some extent. It's easier and most profitable though to sell it in an unprocessed form, either the live plants or the dried product. Not only that, there are so many different microclimates and soil compositions here. You know how that affects grapes. It's the same with lavender."

Savvy gave her a tight smile. She knew all too well what Elizabeth meant, but she avoided getting into wine conversations whenever possible. Too often, they led back to her family.

"So yes, it's true," she continued. "Lots of folks grow a few plants. Some DIY types even experiment with blending small batches of essential oils for themselves, but here at our store we have high standards for consistency, packaging, and the like. We have a reputation for quality. You understand."

Lavender was way more complicated than she'd thought. Every answer spawned another question.

Esteban came over, and Savvy introduced him.

"I'll take a couple of Anne's bundles, and this Welsh perfume," said Savvy. "And another perfume for comparison, using the—what did you call it? Intermediate?

"Intermedia. The Dutch one. Also called lavandin." She laughed. "Sometimes even I get overwhelmed."

"Oh—and Anne's card, if you have an extra?"

Early the next morning, Savvy called to see if she and Esteban could get in to visit the lavender ranch.

"Yes, this is Anne Rathmell," said the voice on the phone.

"Hi, Anne. We've never met, but I got your name from Elizabeth Hull at Smells Like Napa."

"I'm sorry, we're not interested in wholesaling anywhere else. We're not real farmers. Just people looking for peace and quiet who got lucky"—she laughed drily—"depending on your point of view—with the perfect piece of land for growing lavender."

"I'm not a retailer. The reason I'm calling is because I'm interested in learning more about your still."

There was a pause. "Unfortunately, I can't really help you there, either. It came with the property. It's been sitting there for ten years, collecting dust. To tell you the truth, I'm not even sure if it works."

"That's okay. I've been trying to educate myself online about the distillation process, but that's not the same as actually being able to see a real still up close—to touch one. I thought if I could take a look at yours, it might help."

"Well . . ." Anne hesitated.

Please say yes.

"I didn't catch your name, earlier."

"Savvy."

"Savvy?" Anne's chuckle held a semblance of doubt. "As in smart and savvy?"

Oh, she was savvy, all right. So savvy that the one and only time she'd had sex, she hadn't taken precautions.

"Are you there?" asked Anne.

"As in Savvy St. Pierre." Savvy held her breath. You never knew which way that would go.

Dead air filled the phone. "The wine family? Oh my, Lucas and I were just reading about—never mind. Um . . . I suppose it might be all right if you stopped out sometime."

Excitement swelled like a balloon in Savvy's chest.

"It can't be until the end of the month, though."

The balloon deflated a little.

"I'm collaborating on a project so I'm afraid my timeline isn't very flexible. Still interested?"

What choice did she have? "Sure. I don't want to be an inconvenience."

"No inconvenience, but we've got some travel planned. Could you come out, say, the thirtieth?"

Today was only the ninth, but what could she say? Anne Rathmell was doing her a favor. "That would be fine."

"What time of day were you thinking?"

"Say, around six?" If she left right after work, she could be there in twenty-five minutes.

"It'll be getting dark by then. Are you sure you don't want to come when it's light out? You'll be able to see the property better."

And miss work? She only paused a moment. "Four, then?" It wouldn't matter if she left early, just once.

"Four sounds great. I'll be waiting for you, April thirtieth."

"Oh—Ms. Rathmell? May I bring a friend along?"

"I don't see why not. I'll leave the gate open."

Chapter 19

At her desk, Savvy sipped her smoothie and tried not to grimace at the taste. After a couple of weeks of tacos and burgers with the partners, the stressful trial she'd assisted on had finally been decided in favor of her firm's client. She was overdue for a healthy lunch.

As she sipped, she set aside her briefs. Scrolling through page after page of information about perfume blending, she pressed her fingers to her temple. Why did all her interests have to be so complicated? And why was she always in such a hurry to squeeze in everything there was to know, in as short amount of time as possible?

She'd downloaded some books to her iPad. Titles like *The A-Z Guide to Perfumes* and *Discover the Alchemy of Scent*.

But digesting all those books would take forever. What she was looking for was a crash course in how to train as a "nose" while still being a lawyer. Her lunch hour had already turned into her lunch ninety minutes.

From the myriad choices Google gave her, she selected one Lawrence van Horne, "prominent master perfumer and director of the New York Perfumery School," and shot him an email asking him to contact her. She sighed after she pressed send, realizing she'd still have to settle for cramming from books until Van Horne got back to her. Assuming he ever did.

"Savvy?"

She jumped a mile when Robert Witmer poked his head in her door.

"Sorry, didn't mean to startle you."

He slid into her lone visitor's chair, propping a wingtip on his opposite knee. So far, her boss had taken a hands-off approach. But she knew sooner or later he'd want an update.

"You didn't startle me!" she shrilled. *Click, click, click* went her laptop, as she closed tab after tab of perfume pages. *Jeesh!* When had its keys become so audible?

"How's it going?"

"Fine!" Evidence destroyed, she sat up perkily, crossed her arms atop her yellow legal pad, and gave him her winningest smile.

"Now, you know I'm not a micromanager."

She scowled. "No, I know you're not, Mr. Witmer. Definitely not."

"I'm a firm believer in giving my people some head. Er, their rope. Their head, some rope. You know what I mean. Do you feel like you're being micromanaged?"

"No, sir! Not at all. I'm fine with the way you're, um, giving me head."

He gave a curt nod. "Good. Even so, it has been a while since we touched base on the NTI deal. I wanted to check in, see how things are going."

She cleared her throat. The trial had been a major distraction for a while, but she knew this moment was coming. "And I'm so glad you did! Things are going great. So great." She scooted her chair farther forward, inadvertently spying a week's worth of mindless doodles filling every square inch of her pad: *Esteban Morales* written up one side and down the other, surrounded by the most elementary sketches of daisies and roses. Unlike Meri, she couldn't draw worth a darn.

She adjusted her arms accordingly.

"So did Mr. Morales ever get back to you on your initial offer?"

"Ah, yes. Yes he did, as a matter of fact."

Robert turned over a palm. "And?"

"Well, it seems that offer wasn't quite in line with their way of thinking."

"Would you mind elaborating?"

Her smile faded. "One-point-five wasn't enough."

He gave her a blank look, then made a rolling motion with his hand. "So, what happened? Did they counter?"

"Not exactly."

"What exactly did they say, Savvy?"

She couldn't tell him they were deadlocked and she hadn't yet figured a way to fix it. And no way could she admit that she was starting to care more about the Moraleses' son than the Moraleses' land.

"Well, they said, you know, that one-point-five wasn't going to be enough, but they didn't say how much *would* be enough, so I went ahead and offered them one-point-six."

Robert dropped his chin and glared up at her. "With Don Smith's approval, of course."

She mock-grimaced. "Was I supposed to get NTI's approval before I did that?"

Robert sighed and raised his brow. "Er, yeah. That would've been the thing to do."

"My mistake." She held her breath, walking a tightrope waiting for Robert's reaction. Sometimes the smart thing to do was act dumb, even though he had to know she couldn't be that ignorant.

He rose and paced the length of her desk. "Now don't panic," he said, rubbing the back of his neck, talking more to himself than to her. "NTI didn't really expect Morales to take their first offer, anyway. Matter of fact, their first counter probably would've been one-point-seven-five. What'd they say?"

"Hm?" She bought time to invent a response.

"What. Did. The Moraleses. Say."

"Umm . . . they haven't got back to me yet. They're still thinking about it." She nodded like a bobblehead doll, her lips a tight smile. "Still considering."

Abruptly, Robert paused mid-pace and cocked his head, his eye having been caught by the curlicues on her pad. His neck craned slightly.

Savvy leaned farther forward, unstacking her forearms to cover more area, all the while keeping her eyes focused on Robert's face, willing him to look up.

Robert's chin jutted out and his eyeballs swiveled downward, angling to see exactly what was on that pad.

Savvy lowered herself until her thorax practically lay on the table. *Oh, for big boobs.*

Finally, his eyes returned to hers. "Savvy, may I give you a word of wisdom? Not micromanaging or anything. Just fatherly advice, the same thing I'd give my own daughter."

She gave him a virtuous look. "Of course."

"Don't get caught kissing men in parking lots. Even if you are trying to get them to make a deal."

He turned on his heel and walked out.

When she was sure he was gone, Savvy shut her eyes, whooshed out the breath she hadn't known she'd been holding, and let her forehead fall to the desk.

Chapter 20

"Listen to this," said Savvy, reading off her phone. "You put the lavender into the boiler canister, and the steam comes out through a hose and is captured in this vertical tube called a condenser, which separates the liquid, called hydrosol, from the oil. And that's it," she said, leaning across the table in her enthusiasm. Even her thick lenses couldn't hide the sparkle in her eyes. "That's all there is to it! That's the basic process of distillation." She popped her forkful of calamari into her mouth.

Reluctantly, Esteban tore his eyes away from her plump lips and tried to keep his mind on why he'd brought her here, to Bodega, tonight.

Last time they were together at the lavender store, bad as he wanted to rip that dress right off of her and do her in the truck bed, he'd driven her straight home. After the coast, he needed her to realize what he wanted from her went beyond sex.

She'd sounded thrilled when he'd called a few days later to set up tonight's date, squeezed in between all his preparations for opening day.

A twinge of guilt nagged him at his real intention. Yeah, he wanted to see her again. She was all he thought about from dawn to dusk, while he worked the farm. And after dusk? Not one night had gone by that he hadn't lost sleep over the vision of her straddling him on the sand. Her furrowed brow, her parted lips as he drove into her again and again.

But their sex on the beach wasn't all that haunted him. There was something else that kept him up, and not in a good way.

"There's so much to learn!" said Savvy, swallowing a sip of wine, the burgundy liquid swirling perilously close to the rim of her glass when she set it back down.

"I know. I can't believe the price that grower who supplies Smells Like Napa is getting for her Hidcote bundles at wholesale. That's got to be over a five hundred percent profit margin."

That wasn't the only thing he had trouble believing. How was it that he, Esteban Morales, was with Sauvignon St. Pierre? The leaf green she was wearing tonight made her rosy cheeks look even pinker. She didn't seem to notice the attention they were attracting in the restaurant. The heads turning, the whispering. Especially that *güey* with the man bag sitting over at the bar who wouldn't stop glancing their way.

Maybe she was used to it, but he wasn't. Were they talking about how beautiful she was? Her famous, yet notorious father? Or were they wondering why one of Napa Valley's most eligible bachelorettes was hanging out with a truck farmer?

"Let's go visit that ranch together."

Esteban thought as he swigged his draft. "You can't just show up at someone's ranch and ask for a tour."

"It's all set up. Anne Rathmell's expecting us."

"What did you say to her?"

"That I overheard her conversation at Smells Like Napa, and I was interested in looking at her still and my farmer friend wanted to see which lavender varieties grow best on her land."

"And just like that, she invited us over."

She shrugged. "Just like that."

The server set down their salads.

Esteban was starting to realize that things moved faster in Savvy's world than they did in his. She had this confidence hardwired into her that she could make things happen with a click of her heels.

Meanwhile, he was still trying to come to grips with all that had happened in the past couple of weeks since she'd first set foot on his property.

"So, are you in? Will you come with me?"

Like he had it in him to say no. "I'll come."

She clapped her hands. "This is going to be so much fun, learning all about lavender together."

That was exactly what he'd been thinking. That, and about banging her like a screen door in a hurricane. Inside his Levi's, his balls tightened.

But there wouldn't be any more careless banging anytime soon.

Going forward, things were going to be different. She wasn't just another *chula.*

He needed to come clean about that damn counteroffer. Now.

"There's something we need to talk about."

With an easy smile, she tilted her head, twisting a diamond earring. "You look so serious."

He took a preparatory breath. "I told you the real estate deal was dead because that's what I believed. But those weren't Padre's exact words." He looked her straight in the eye. "He didn't say he wouldn't take *any* offer."

Smile gone, she stared back at him, unblinking.

"That is, not exactly. He told me to counter at two million."

"Two million?" She dropped her fingers from her earring and leaned toward him.

He let it sink in.

"I figured no way was that going to happen. I was still blown away that someone thought it was worth one-point-five. That's why—especially with the language barrier and all—I decided on my own to simplify things. Cut through the bull and tell you there was no sense in negotiating any more."

She leaned across the table. "Wait. So what you're saying is that it's not that your land is so very precious that your father won't let it go at any price. He's holding out for more money."

"No!" He looked around to be sure no one had overheard, then lowered his voice. "No. That's not it. What I told you is true. Padre only pulled two million out of his hat as a symbol. Two mil, ten mil . . . those are all just numbers to someone like him. He can't even conceive of them, in real life. He was trying to make the point that no amount of money would ever be enough. That money has nothing to do with it."

Savvy sat back. "I don't know what to say. Two million is twenty-five percent over the current offer. I can't imagine NTI would go that high."

"So you agree then. There's no sense in even presenting it."

She flattened her palms on the tablecloth. "NTI hired our firm to buy that land. Now that you've told me about this, I think I'm obligated to share it with them."

A tiny arrow of panic zinged through him.

"Can you see it from my point of view?"

What could he say?

"I'll need to get the offer in writing. Do you think that'll be a problem?"

He ran a hand through his hair, exhaling heavily. "Padre won't like it, but now that he's made the offer verbally, he'll feel obliged to back it up."

"Let me guess. Honor, right?" She smiled wryly. "I'll draw up the paperwork. Tell him not to stress too much. I doubt it'll go any further."

"Thanks for dinner," said Savvy as they strolled through the Bodega parking lot to Esteban's truck.

He should be thanking *her.* The more time he spent with Savvy, the more he liked her. Now that he'd told Savvy about Padre's extreme offer and she'd agreed that it wasn't likely to go anywhere, he felt like a weight had been taken off his back. He wrapped an arm around her shoulders and pulled her close.

In the Chevy, she took off her glasses and scooted across the seat toward him. In the process, her not-black dress slid up. He glanced over at her naked eyes boring into his, then down at the finest pair of knees in Napa. *Caramba.*

She reached around his neck with both hands, kissing his cheek. His temple. His ear. He lifted his chin, relishing the soft velvet of her lips forging a trail across his skin.

Ay, Savvy. He couldn't resist kissing her back.

"I love being with you," she murmured in her proper, prep school tones.

"Me too," he managed. He cleared his throat. They should get going.

She started kissing him again and it didn't feel like a good-night kiss.

Now, before his *verga* put a dent in the steering wheel . . .

A blinding flash of white light flooded her window. *"Oh!"* Savvy screamed and pressed into his shoulder, covering her face with her hands.

¡¿Qué chingados es eso?! Esteban was out of the truck in a split second, leaving his door hanging wide open. The *güey* with the man bag was running back toward the restaurant.

Within a half dozen strides, Esteban grabbed his shirt, spun him around, and pulled back his fist. "What are you doing, *pendejo?*"

The man shrank, shielding his face with his arm. "Nothing! I'm not doing anything! Let me go!"

Esteban heard crunching on pavement and felt a hand clutch his arm. "Stop it!" said Savvy. "Let him go, Esteban! He's just a paparazzo. He's not worth it."

"Where's your camera?" demanded Esteban, drawing back a little farther. The *güey* whimpered, tucking his face into the crook of his elbow.

Just then the silhouette of a couple came around the corner of the building, halting mid-step when they witnessed the scene. The man thrust a sheltering arm across his date.

"Please!" man-bag dude screamed. "Help! Somebody help me!"

"Let him go," Savvy pleaded, tugging urgently at Esteban's arm with both hands, her voice lowered. "C'mon, before you're the one in trouble!"

In disgust, Esteban dropped him. He fell to his side, then scrambled to his feet and ran away.

"La madre que te parió!," Esteban called to his back. *Gracias a Dios,* Savvy didn't know Spanish.

Chapter 21

Late the next evening, tired as Savvy was, she couldn't sleep. Papa made a detour on his way to his study when he saw her sitting at the breakfast table.

He looked askance at the bag of cookies and the tall glass of milk. "I thought French women did not snack," he said, kissing her cheek.

"I'm hungry," she said, letting the excess drip off her third Oreo before popping it into her mouth. She downed it, adding, "Besides, I'm an American. Born right here in Napa County, remember? We Americans are actually known for our snacking." She gave him a crumby black grin and inserted her hand back into the bag.

Papa raised one eyebrow. "So it seems."

He lowered himself into the chair next to her. "How is my little lawyer?"

Why now, when the NTI land deal was at an impasse? Wasn't it a little late for him to develop an interest in Savvy's job? Except for the time she'd gotten into the gifted program back in elementary school, he'd never paid the slightest bit of attention to her classes, her report cards. In fact, Papa would probably have been fine with all three of his daughters lounging by the pool the rest of their lives. So it was kind of ironic that they'd all three ended up passionately involved in one kind of work or another. Then again, maybe not, when you considered Papa's own workaholic tendencies. Maman's too, come to think of it. She'd left for L.A. to make a movie only weeks after Meri was born.

Savvy wasn't falling for it. "I'm doing well, Papa."

"My compliments on the photograph," Papa said, as if it were an afterthought.

Savvy froze, cookie poised, dripping with milk. "Pardon?" she asked warily.

"Why, for making use of all of the weapons in your arsenal in pursuit of your goal."

She licked off her milk moustache and frowned. "What are you talking about?"

"My bright daughter, using her feminine wiles to snare her prey. What was it Machiavelli said? 'Keep your friends close, and your enemies closer.' "

She snorted as she dipped another cookie. "Machiavelli was an unethical, self-centered bastard. Where do you think the expression 'Old Nick' came from for the devil? Niccolò, Papa. Good ol' Niccolò Machiavelli."

He sat back with a confused, hurt look. "All Machiavelli said was that the truth is better than an abstract ideal." He made lofty air quotes. " 'The ends justify the means.' Why do you think he has been the model of successful businessmen down through the ages?"

Impatiently, Savvy shook her head and peered into the bag. All gone. "What's this all about?"

He gave her a look. "You have not seen the story?"

"What stor—" *The paparazzo.* Wiping her fingers, she rose to retrieve her phone from over on the counter and started scrolling as she walked absently back to the table. Before she got there, her feet stopped moving.

Wine Heiresses Behaving Badly

"In the Spring a young man's fancy lightly turns to thoughts of love." So said Alfred, Lord Tennyson.

Apparently not much has changed since the nineteenth century. As it was in England, so it is in Napa.

Which might make an excellent argument as to why legal eagle and Domaine St. Pierre heiress Sauvignon was seen cozying up to the driver of a red Chevy Silverado parked behind Bodega on a recent balmy April night. Said driver, with his long, flowing locks, looked more like a Romance-era gentleman farmer than the typical Napa bracero.

The aptly named Savvy, eldest daughter of Xavier St. Pierre, became the first female associate of Witmer, Robinson and Scott soon after graduating with honors from Boston University School of Law. She and her sisters, Chardonnay and Merlot, guard their privacy, shunning the spotlight and only rarely commenting on social media. Yet they seem to share an uncanny knack for being found in compromising positions—a trait they inherited from their colorful parents.

Mr. St. Pierre is as famous for his cult cabernets as he is infamous for his ever-changing cast of companions since the death of his wife, Academy Award–winning actress Lily d'Amboise. As to whether the couple were separated when she left town with an Argentine winemaker, only to die with him days later in the wreck of his Maserati, the jury is still out.

Following the tragic demise of their mother, the daughters were whisked out of the public eye into exclusive eastern prep schools. Now they're back, and wine country residents thirsty for sightings haven't been disappointed....

The Oreos almost came back up.

"Papa! I am one hundred percent not using Esteban for ... *that!*"

Papa's brows went together. "Why such a strong reaction? You are misunderstanding. I am not reprimanding you. *Au contraire, ma chére.* I am giving you credit."

"Well, you're wrong! That's not what I'm doing with Esteban. I like him. It's real."

Papa threw up his hands. "Fine," he harrumphed. "I see that is your story, and you are sticking to her." With a disdainful glance at the empty cookie bag, he strode away, leaving Savvy sucking cookie residue out of her teeth.

"Who are you sticking to?" asked Meri, entering from another room.

Savvy huffed, "Papa out and out accused me of sleeping with Esteban Morales to get him to sell his land. Can you believe him? Like we're just some sort of—I don't know, hook-up buddies."

"So much for Bodega being Stan-free," Meri replied in the droll way she had.

Savvy's palms went up. "Is that all you can say in my defense?"

Meri poured a glass of water and plopped down beside her. "*Is that why you slept with him?*" Her eyes bored ruthlessly into Savvy's.

"No!" *Yes*. That had been her initial intention, even though it hadn't turned out that way.

Inside her silk robe, Meri lifted a shoulder. "Then don't worry about it. You know Papa. Tomorrow there'll be another scandal, and he'll forget all about this one." She drank the rest of her water and poured another to take up to her room. "G'night." She padded away on bare feet.

If Meri only knew. Scandal was all Savvy could think about, now that her period was late.

To say that her cycle was regular was an understatement. She knew when her period would start with the same certainty that she knew Justice Sotomayor would always rule on the liberal side.

Today was the day.

But there'd been nothing. Not one drop of red. Not a trace.

She invented a bunch of excuses to calm her racing heart:

Human bodies weren't machines.

No one was regular *all* the time.

She'd been stressed lately.

She was getting older.

Maybe hormones played a part. After all, she'd just discovered her sexuality, hadn't she? In spite of her worry, a small smile played on her lips at the thought of what Esteban had done to her . . . all the long-submerged feelings he'd awakened. That was enough to make any woman's hormones go cuckoobananapants.

The footsteps returned.

Meri poked her head around the entrance to the kitchen to see Savvy still sitting in the same place. She tilted her head sympathetically, came over, and put her arms around Savvy. "It'll be okay. I'm going to bed. You should, too. Love you."

Much as Savvy hated to admit it, Papa was right. Using Esteban for her own gain was exactly what she had had planned. Workaholism wasn't the only thing she'd inherited from Papa. She was a Machiavellian. She'd thought she had such lofty ethics coming out of law school. So above the stereotypical lawyer antics. If she had to resort to sleeping with people to win cases, maybe that meant she wasn't cut out to be an attorney.

Then again, maybe that meant she *was*.

"Love you, too," she murmured to the empty room.

Chapter 22

"*In fifty yards, turn right,*" said the GPS.

"Here?" Esteban wondered aloud at an unmarked dirt road leading straight up through hills resembling humpback whales.

He pulled the truck off Napa Road and shifted into second to make it up the steep grade.

"*Arriving at destination.*"

At the open gate, Savvy peered behind them through the truck's back window. "Wow," she breathed.

He twisted around to see the late afternoon sun reflected off a puddle of blue. "That's the bay!"

Their eyes met, sealing the moment in time.

"Look at the house," she cried when the square, Tuscan-style stucco with the orange tile roof came into view.

A woman in jeans with long silver hair came out to greet them. Savvy introduced Esteban.

"I think I recognize you," she said to him with a wry smile.

"From the lavender store?"

"Among other places." At Savvy's puzzled expression, she added, "I spend a lot of time on the computer."

Anne led them behind the house where there were olive groves and a swath of land that had been tilled, once upon a time. "All my husband and I were looking for was a quiet place to write and paint. We got quiet, all right. Sometimes during the day the only sounds are the cattle lowing at the next ranch. At night, you can hear the coyotes howling up on the ridge. But after a couple of years we started feeling guilty about leaving those fat olives hanging there, begging to be picked. So now we hire someone to harvest them and send them out to be pressed. The lavender has completely gotten away from us, even though we did nothing to encourage it. It's never been touched by chemicals, as far as we know."

Esteban thrust his hands in his pockets and eyeballed the tangled field of last year's crop that had long gone to seed. "How many acres you got here?"

"Eight." She half laughed. "We're from Cupertino. Eight acres sounded manageable when we first bought the place. What did we know?"

He crouched to scoop up a handful of crumbly soil, letting it sift through his fingers.

"'Sandy loam.' So says the guy from the UC Cooperative Extension." She shrugged.

What I'd give for dirt like this, he thought.

"We're right on the Sonoma–Napa line. We've got dry, hot summers and cold winters. Our fruit trees love it."

"And you?" Savvy asked.

Her lips curled in a crooked smile. "Some days it's a little more extreme than what we signed up for. We're used to living in a city. It can be a little isolated out here."

"Want to look at the distillery?" She turned toward an outbuilding, Savvy close on her heels.

Esteban seemed rooted to the ground. "Okay if I wander around some? I see you've got a peach orchard."

"Plums, too," said Anne. "There's nothing like fresh plum jam."

But the orchards weren't what interested him most. He walked into the middle of the rough field of Hidcote, the species and variety that had made up the bundles Savvy had bought at the shop in Napa, and inhaled the sweet, clean air.

A half hour later, he saw the women exit the distillery from where he stood atop the highest ridge, looking down on the roof of the farmhouse where a glass conservatory off the back opened up to a kitchen garden and a three-car garage.

"How's the view?" Savvy waved and called to him. There was a lighthearted quality to her voice. She must have liked what she'd seen of the still.

"Primo." He breathed in the southern wind, taking one last look at the undulating landscape beneath a dusky blue sky, memorizing the scene. Blinking low in the west of the celestial sphere were the three stars of Orion's belt, the winter constellation, almost gone now that spring was here.

"You can see five counties from up there," shouted Anne.

He turned in a slow circle. Starting in the east, there was Napa, followed by Solano to the southeast. Directly south, the bay water broke up the land mass. On its other shore was Marin. Sonoma fell to the west, and Lake, in the north.

Like Savvy said: *Wow.*

Fortified with Madre's baked eggs and chorizo, Esteban carried his coffee mug out to the greenhouse bright and early Friday, squinting against the rising sun. Madre was getting ready for eight o'clock Mass. Padre had just left for the diner to have breakfast with his *amigos.*

Last night's dreams of Savvy still swirled in Esteban's head. From the back of his Chevy, he loaded up the first wheelbarrow full of Rathmell Ranch lavender. Anne had offered to let him dig up as many plants as he wanted after he'd told her about his struggle to grow the herb. She'd even shown him where to find some discarded plastic pots in her barn.

He'd considered building a whole new raised bed, but that didn't make sense. If he was going to do this, he needed to go all the way, and he couldn't make a raised bed to cover all five acres. All lavender liked well-drained, slightly alkaline soil, and there was no place on his property like that. He'd have to settle for amending what soil he did have. It could work.

Savvy had saved his life.

She'd given him something worth more than all the land in the world—her virginity. Him, Esteban Morales. In the month since, there hadn't been an hour that didn't fill him with awe.

He wanted to give her the respect due a queen.

He wheeled his young plants and supplies into an open area with full sun and good air circulation, his eye on the sky. The waxing crescent moon was in Scorpio, a water sign. No better time for planting.

He set down the wheelbarrow and measured the pH of the clay. Six-point-five. Some lime mixed in with the bone meal and composted manure might bring it up to neutral. He started to work on a bed, spading in his customized mixture as he went.

Before long, he heard footsteps and turned to see Madre wearing a skirt, her cloth purse slung over her shoulder.

"I'm leaving now. Are you sure you don't want to come?"

"This is my church." He indicated his surroundings with his chin. "The earth. The trees." He grunted, booting the spade into the dense ground. "The sky."

"You haven't been to Mass in a long while," Madre lamented.

He scooped out another shovelful of dirt. "And not a single day goes by when I'm not thankful for what we have. This land has never failed to provide for us yet."

Why should he invent sins purely to have something to confess to the priest? He had never intentionally hurt a single living thing: plant, animal, or human. Just minded his business, respected his parents, and worked each day until he couldn't work any more.

"And who do you think made all those things?"

Huffing with his efforts, he gulped the last of his coffee, tossed his mug onto the ground, and wiped his mouth with his sleeve as he watched her stomp off to her car, shaking her head.

Besides, he couldn't go to church right now. Not when his thoughts were full of Sauvignon St. Pierre, naked on a rocky, windswept beach.

She'd been totally pure until he'd left his mark on her. Maybe he was *too* earthy. He found himself wanting to mate with her in every sense of the word. Build a home with her. Plant his seed in her. Slay a mastodon and drag it home for her to eat . . .

Working and dreaming made the hours slip by.

"Welcome to your new home," he whispered to each plant as he firmed down the soil around it. "Settle in good now, you hear?"

Then he stood back and looked at his handiwork, knowing deep down that if these robust specimens didn't take root here, no lavender ever would.

Chapter 23

Savvy was tempted to leave work early—again. Maybe because it was Friday. Or was it spring fever? After the oppressive winter, the weather was finally gorgeous. From her office window, daffodils teased her, nodding their heads in the grass along the border of the office park.

While the firm's partners hadn't exactly broadcast that they were blowing off the rest of the day to play golf, the white belts and khakis they'd worn to work had made any pronouncement superfluous. Mid-morning, the men had simply vanished.

For about five seconds, Savvy wondered if she should feel snubbed at not having been invited to tag along. Really though, why bother? She was the only female lawyer in the firm. The next youngest had at least twenty years on her. Not only that, she'd sucked at every sport she'd ever tried. Okay, she could swim, but it wasn't pretty.

With the partners gone, the whole suite seemed to take on a more relaxed air. Maybe she could use this time to finally make some headway with the other women, as soon as she tied up some loose ends. She proofread the document she'd just typed and sent it to the printer in another room.

On her way to retrieve her copies, the sound of feminine chatter coming from the break room buoyed her hopes. She made a detour in time to see Karen popping another K-Cup in the Keurig, and Sylvia waiting her turn.

"Guess it's just us girls this afternoon," Savvy said, pasting on her best Miss Congeniality smile.

Midsentence, Karen's mouth clamped shut. Sylvia's eyes filled with resentment.

All righty, then. There were at least two people who wouldn't miss her if she bugged out early.

She tried to look at the bright side. At least the assistants weren't pretending to like her, and then dissing her to her back. This way, she knew for certain that anything and everything she did would be duly reported.

She grabbed a handful of hard candy from a dish. All she'd put in her stomach that day was that disgusting kale drink.

Back at her desk, she found herself watching the clock. Peering out the window yet again at the clouds drifting by, she worried her lower lip, considering. She was salaried, not hourly. It wasn't like she needed permission. But cutting out early two days in a row was no way for a junior associate to make an impression.

Still, it *was* Friday.

She called Esteban on her way home, and he asked her to go out later. While they talked, she thought about her last conversation with her boss, racking her brain to figure out some way she could make Esteban's father see that that offer on his land was a boon, not something to be dismissed out of hand. She still didn't get the Moraleses' reaction. Most people would jump at the chance to painlessly unload a property that only afforded a meager living, in exchange for never having to worry about work or money again.

As she pulled into Domaine St. Pierre, she realized she was starving—and tired. Maybe it was a good thing she'd gone home early after all. It was all she could do to haul her bagful of work up the steps and into the house.

She entered the kitchen to the smell of fish baking.

"Salut," sang Jeanne. "You are never the first one home from work. You are surprising me every day, *ma petite chou,"* she said from over at the island, where she tossed a green salad.

Normally Savvy found it touching when Jeanne called her "my little cabbage." But today, the endearment was overshadowed by the way the island was swirling around like a kaleidoscope. The awful kale drink tasted even worse going down the second time, mixed with hard candy. Her knees felt like jelly. At the sound of her steadying hand smacking down on the edge of the breakfast table, Jeanne looked up.

Savvy's fingers curled over the table edge as stars danced before her eyes.

In a flash, the cook was at her side, one hand on her back, the other supporting her elbow.

"Mon Dieu. Sit. Sit down."

Savvy dropped into a chair with a *thunk*, her black satchel falling over on the kitchen tile, documents streaming out of it.

"Are you ill?" Jeanne's face was the picture of concern as she bent over Savvy, cupping her cheeks.

"No. I don't know. I felt dizzy, all of a sudden."

"Stay there. I will get you a drink."

"I forgot to eat today. That's all."

Thirty-one days since Salt Point. Forty-five since her last period. She didn't need a clear head to figure those numbers. She recalculated them daily. No—*hourly.*

"You look like a ghost," Jeanne said, standing over her to ensure she drank the full glass of water she brought. "I told you before, you work too hard. Go upstairs and lie down, and I will bring you something."

It wasn't in Savvy to argue. As she dragged herself out of the room and across the foyer to the stairs, she heard Jeanne muttering a scolding in French. "I heard that," she called out over her shoulder.

She awoke sometime later to answer her phone, still in her work clothes, the bedroom in shadow. A silver tray of tea and toast sat on the bedside table.

"What time do you want me to pick you up?" asked Esteban, when she answered.

"What time is it?" She rubbed her eyes. "I can't remember the last time I fell asleep during the daytime."

"Seven-thirty."

With an effort, she hoisted herself up on an elbow. "Um . . ." The thought of eating anything other than toast made her stomach somersault.

Jeanne walked briskly into the bedroom with a cup and saucer. Did she have a mom-cam, with that timing?

"You are not to even *think* of going out," Jeanne said, loud enough to be overheard by whomever was on the phone.

Warily, Savvy watched Jeanne fuss . . . replacing the untouched cold tea with the hot cup, motioning to get Savvy to roll over so she could turn down the duvet. Not since Savvy had had that bad stomach flu back when she was six had she seen Jeanne act this way. *Ugh.* The thought of that made her stomach flip again.

"Who's that?" asked Esteban through the phone.

Like a beached whale, Savvy let Jeanne roll her back over, sighing as the duvet was pulled up and tucked in around her. She had to admit, it felt good to be mothered occasionally, even if she *was* full grown.

"That would be Jeanne . . ." was all she dared say within the tyrant's hearing.

"Esteban?" Jeanne asked Savvy pointedly.

When Savvy glared at her like the madwoman she was, Jeanne took the phone.

"Here is Jeanne, *mon chér.* Mademoiselle Sauvignon is too tired to come out tonight. I am very sorry, but there it is. Give your mother my regards. Good-bye." With that, she matter-of-factly handed the phone back and left the room.

Savvy tucked another pillow behind her head and chatted with him for a few more minutes, the tea settling her stomach enough to make her not-sick claim sound almost convincing. Esteban told her he'd be busy all day tomorrow getting ready for the opening of the Napa farmers' market the following weekend, but he wanted to take her hiking on Sunday, if the weather held.

"Bye," she cooed finally, the phone wedged between her ear and her pillow.

"Bye."

"Don't have fun without me," she pouted.

"Not a chance," replied her gentle giant.

So. Sunday it would be. She had 'til then to figure out how to make him see the obvious advantages of accepting NTI's offer, and then get him to convince his dad of same.

Bwawp! Bwap-bwap!

Esteban turned from his gray-green shrubs tucked into their new earthen beds to see Tomas's pickup coming up the lane, followed by a hand waving out the window of the latest-model Jeep Wrangler.

"*¿Que pasa,* my friend?" said Tomas. He slammed his door and strode up the lane to meet him.

They shook hands, Esteban clapping Tomas's arm for good measure. "Not much. Just checking on the lavender."

"Still? How long you going to keep beating your head against the wall, man?"

Esteban's hopes were up this morning. "Got some exceptional plants from a place over on the county line. I feel good about it this time."

Tomas shook his head. "I hope the parentals appreciate what kinda son they got."

How could Esteban make people like Tomas and Savvy understand that what drove him to farm was more than merely a desire to be a good son? His passion to put his own stamp on the property he'd someday inherit? To make it his own?

"What's going on with you two?" Esteban said, changing the subject.

"George and I just came from the dealership. I gave him a ride to pick up his new toy. He had to stop and show it off to you."

"Hey there, E!"

They sauntered down to where their mutual friend had jumped out of his Jeep. George grinned and slapped a proud palm down on its hood.

"She's a beauty," said Esteban, slowly circling the vehicle.

"Four-wheel drive, V6, AT tires, seven-speaker sound system . . ."

"Sweet. Making journeyman's paying off, I see."

George's chest puffed out a little. "Not doing too bad." He gestured toward the vegetable gardens. "You ever get tired of playing Old MacDonald here, let me know. I'll hook you up," he said, teasing him the way only an old friend could get away with.

It wasn't the first time George had offered to get him a job at the utility company. Esteban had always dismissed the idea out of hand. Still, he had to admit it was decent of George to offer. "Four-year apprenticeship, is it?" he asked, to show his appreciation.

George shrugged. "Gotta start somewhere. For no college, pay's pretty damn good, even for an apprentice. I started at thirty-four an hour, and now I'm making forty-two."

"They have to pay you good. Wouldn't catch me climbing those poles, grabbing those high-voltage wires," put in Tomas.

George said, "We can always use a hard worker like you, E. One word from me, you're in like Flynn."

"Thanks. I'll keep it in mind." It was his stock response.

"What's going on this weekend?" George asked.

"Getting ready for the market. Opening day is only two weeks away."

Tomas raised his chin in acknowledgment. "Long couple of weeks for your family, eh?"

"Lot of work, but it's all good. First day's always special. Big crowds, music, and special events for the kids." It had always been one of his favorite times of year.

"It's a great event for the community." After Napa Valley Community College Tomas had gone on to the police academy before getting his job as a deputy sheriff for the county.

George tossed his head toward his new vehicle. "I'm taking her out tomorrow to see how she does off-road. Tomas said he's riding along. Want to come?"

Esteban grimaced. "Man, sounds great, but I already made plans for Sunday."

"Work?"

Sheepishly, Esteban shook his head. "Not this time."

George slid him a sideways look. "Hey. That true what I heard?"

"What'd you hear?"

"You were at Bodega with one of the St. Pierre sisters last week?"

Esteban couldn't restrain his shit-eating grin. "Could be."

George smacked Esteban a high-five that turned into a rugged, congratulatory handclasp. "You fucking kidding me?" He looked at Tomas. "How do you like that? Dude hits the big time without telling us."

"How long's that been going on?" asked Tomas with a look in his eye that made Esteban vaguely uncomfortable. As if Tomas had just pulled him over for speeding and was debating whether or not to search his vehicle.

Esteban shrugged. "Not long."

His friends sized him up, digesting the surprising news.

"That's . . . cool," said Tomas.

"All right, well, if you're sure you can't go with us, we'll do it again another time. I'm out of here."

"See you tomorrow," said Tomas.

"You've heard about Xavier St. Pierre," said Tomas as they watched

George drive away with still more honks and waves. "The whole valley has. It's like they say: the rich are different than us."

Esteban looked down for a second before meeting Tomas's eyes. "Guess I'll find out."

"Guess you will," Tomas replied as he headed to his truck. "Take care, buddy," he added, opening his door. "I hope you know what you're getting into."

Chapter 24

"What about this gouda?" Savvy called, her head in the open refrigerator.

"It's good. I only bought it on Friday," replied Jeanne.

Savvy came out holding the package of cheese, making a face. "It smells awful."

Jeanne stepped over and sniffed. "It smells magnificent," she said, sounding somewhat indignant.

Savvy frowned, thinking. There must be something else she could add to the picnic she was packing for the hike. Somehow everything had this perplexing, off odor today. She settled for strawberries, tucking them into the wicker basket alongside the fried chicken and brownies. It'd been nice of Jeanne to whip up some things that would work for Savvy and Esteban's hike, in addition to the meal she was preparing for everyone else in the household.

When the basket was ready to go, she went upstairs to put on the pink sundress she'd borrowed from Meri. She might be pushing the season a little, but with another day of above-average temperatures, this spring was more than making up for the past few months. Besides, she really wanted to wear a dress.

When Esteban had made love to her, he'd awakened something deep in her soul, the likes of which she'd never known. That day on the beach under the warm spring sun, he'd made her feel not just wanted for her body, but *cherished*. Adored. As if she was the very center of his universe. Until that day, Savvy had never even had an inkling of what romantic love was all about. Sure, she loved her sisters. Jeanne loved her, she felt sure. Papa? He'd always kept a roof over her head. All those things paled in comparison to what Esteban did to her.

Though they had their hands all over each other every time they were together—outside his house, in his truck, wherever—they'd still only been together once. She was obsessed with experiencing that delicious feeling of wanting and being wanted again, and a dress could only make it easier.

She spritzed some Chanel No. 5 onto her wrist, and her nose wrinkled. Somehow, nothing smelled the way it was supposed to smell today.

Esteban tried to keep his eyes on the road as he drove north on 29 toward Bothe State Park. Those long, bare legs on the seat next to him were making it mighty hard, though. Because Savvy had put on some flimsy-ass dress to go hiking, like you do. *Pink*, no less. Not only that, she'd switched out the bun to a thick ponytail that she played with as he drove, grasping it hand-over-hand in long, slow strokes. Was the woman trying to kill him?

At least she'd taken his advice and worn sturdy shoes.

"You're quiet today," said Savvy.

"Enjoying the view," he said, clenching the wheel. She smelled great again, soft and sweet, and he could almost feel the warmth emanating from her lithe body.

"Here we are." He parked the truck and grabbed the wicker basketful of food she'd brought, while she carried a blanket.

Everywhere Esteban and Savvy looked along the Redwood Trail, the forest was in bloom. Redwoods and madrone trees were bursting with green and the woods seemed full of hope, rebirth, and growth.

"Violets." Savvy pointed to the flecks of purple dotting the green carpet they walked on. "Do you know, I haven't taken a walk in the woods since I moved back to Cali."

"Did you get outside a lot back east?"

She gave him a sidelong grin. "About the only glimpse of nature I got in Boston was the weeds between the cracks in the sidewalk."

They unpacked their picnic under some towering firs and listened to the water splashing down a rocky creek bed nearby while they ate chicken and sipped their Solo cups of wine.

"How's the Rathmells' lavender adapting?"

Music to his ears. She and Madre were the only people who ever asked. "This sun is the best thing that could happen for them. I think the roots are taking hold already. Might really work this time."

"Yay." From her seat on the blanket, she leaned over to squeeze his bicep. "I can't stop thinking about Anne Rathmell's still. Do you think she would sell it to me? They say the old copper ones are best. Nowadays they're making them out of steel."

"Where would you keep it?"

"What would you think about me keeping it in your greenhouse? That is, if you have room."

If his lavender took off, there would be a still right there on the premises to extract the oil. "I'll *make* room."

Savvy leaned back on her elbows, grinning. "Don't laugh. When I was a little girl, I used to try to make my own perfumes by soaking rose petals in a glass of water. Sometimes I'd add things like grass clippings and crushed grape leaves. After a few days, the top would be covered with mold and our old housekeeper, Hilda, would throw it out. I wonder what ever became of Hilda? I missed out on so much while I was back east.

"What about you?" She eyed him up and down, reclining on the blanket in her pink dress, and he felt a pull in his groin. "Did you always have a fascination with growing things?"

In an effort to distract himself from her legs, he reached over to the bowl of strawberries and popped one into his mouth. "It's like I told you. Farming's in my blood."

Savvy dug in the picnic basket. "Brownie?"

"Thanks." He took a bite. "I don't ever remember thinking that's not what I wanted to do." He polished off the brownie and reached for another. "Farming is a lifestyle. I grew up helping Padre, the same way he helped his dad. That's really the only way to learn it. It's never boring. I love being my own boss, having a flexible schedule. You have to know a little bit of chemistry to understand soil types and fertilizer, even if you're using organic methods, and you have to be a good problem-solver, because there's no one to depend on except yourself."

"What I'm having a hard time wrapping my head around is this. Your dad has already put in an entire lifetime of hard work. Your mom said it's starting to take a toll on his health. Would it really be so wrong to give himself a break—sell his land for a great price? If not for himself, for your mother? After all, if he retires, she retires."

He chuffed. "Madre loves to work as much as he does, if not

more. The market doubles as her social life. I don't know what she'd do without that."

It was important to make her understand the whole picture. "In Mexico, both my grandfathers farmed. Uncle Esteban was the first-born son of his generation. He heard that things were better in America, and he decided to move, to make his family there. He came here as a single man when he was in his early twenties. Too bad, that's where it ended for him. He never had that family."

"That's so sad."

"They say a beautiful woman broke his heart, back in the Michoacán. That's why it wasn't so hard for him to leave."

"He never found someone else?"

Esteban shook his head. "Uncle was a one-woman man. After her, he never dated, never married, never had kids. So when I came along, Grandfather encouraged Padre to follow him to Cali. Uncle and my parents left behind everything . . . family, friends, and homes, to cross the border. You think you missed out on things when you were back east? Imagine never coming back. But they were willing to make that sacrifice for future generations. Grandfather even came up with a name for it. The *Plan Familiar*."

"Family Plan, right? Sorry—if I'd grown up around here, I'd have picked up a lot more Spanish by now."

He nodded. "Our land is what holds us together. Uncle grew Christmas trees, Padre has his fruits and vegetables. Now it's my turn. Each generation can do his own thing on the same piece of ground. You see now?"

Lost in thought, she sipped her wine.

"About that real estate offer," he said.

She lowered her cup and raised her eyes to his.

"Can I ask you something?"

"Ask away."

"If NTI accepts Papa's counter, what's your cut?"

"What?" She scowled, as if she'd never even considered that question.

"What do you get out of this?"

"Six percent of the sale price is standard."

"So, the higher the price it sells for, the more money you make."

"That's generally the way real estate commissions work. In the end, it's all negotiable."

"What would that mean to you?" he asked quietly.

She looked out at some pink rhododendron and thought. "It would mean a lot. Not for the reason you think, though." She poured another inch of wine into her cup and downed it. "I've worked very hard to get where I am. When I was young, all I cared about was getting good grades so I could get into a top law school. Once I got to Boston Law, I spent my first year studying my ass off to qualify for moot court during my second. Then I edited footnotes on boring articles with titles like 'Textualism and Statute Equity' for the law review." She slipped off her glasses and rubbed the bridge of her nose between her eyes. "No wonder these lenses are so freaking thick."

He felt a pang of guilt for busting on her glasses all those times, even if he'd never let on. "What drove you?"

She opened her mouth to say something, then snapped it shut. Finally she said, "What drives anyone? Wanting to make Papa proud, land a good job."

She fingered a yellow violet growing close to the ground. "My goal now is to make partner. To do that, I need to prove I can produce." Then she returned her focus to him. "So, to answer your question, for me, this deal isn't about the money. In fact, I'd probably end up offering to lower my commission, if that's what it would take to make it happen."

Esteban gazed unseeing at his boots, lost in thought.

She touched his leg. "But none of that has anything to do with us, right? Let's put the real estate out of our minds, for now. I don't want it to spoil our day." She tilted her head and smiled softly.

The treetops began to rustle. He looked up. "Wasn't supposed to rain today."

A paper napkin blew a few feet away and Savvy shivered. "I felt a raindrop. I'll start packing up," she said, reaching for the leftover food, stuffing it into the basket. Esteban swooped up the blanket and tossed it over his arm. He reached for Savvy's hand and led her back down the trail at a brisk pace, thinking about love and land and honor, while the wind blew her dress around her legs and the unexpected rain sprinkled their shoulders.

Chapter 25

After another week and a half went by with no response to her email, Savvy couldn't stand it any longer. She called Lawrence Van Horne, the master perfumer.

To her surprise, the man who answered the phone put her through. But her spirits fell again when Van Horne said everything he could to discourage her.

"I appreciate your interest, but I'm afraid what you're asking is impossible—what did you say your name was?"

"Savvy."

"Savvy. I don't know of anyone who would be willing to train you over the Internet, without you coming to New York to learn in person."

"Unfortunately I can't come to New York. I'm a lawyer. I have to stay here and work."

"A lawyer? My dear, you'd best simply stay in California and forget about the perfume world. You'll make a lot more money as a lawyer than you ever will as a nose."

There it was again. Money.

"Are you sure you can't help me? I'm a hard worker. I'm willing to study on my own. Just point me in the right direction, tell me what to read."

"There's only so much you can learn from books. Even working closely under a master, it would take years of training to become a professional nose. You need discipline and patience."

"I'm disciplined. I have patience." She wanted this.

"To begin with, how do I know you're worth training? Without a specific, innate ability, all the training in the world would be a waste of your time and mine."

"I've always had a very acute sense of smell, ever since I was a child. I inherited it from my father. He's a winemaker."

Through the phone came a jaded sigh. "Many people make their own wine. The sense of smell is exceedingly subjective. The only way you could possibly know if you have a trainable nose is to be tested. We do that by having you smell the different scent groups—citrus, floral, wood, and so on—to see if you can distinguish one from another. If you pass that test, the next step is to have you rank scents by intensity, from the faintest to the most concentrated."

"Could you give me the specific instructions for those tests so I can do them on my own, then report back to you?"

She practically heard him rolling his eyes while the seconds ticked by. Her palm was damp from clutching the phone so tightly, and she was aware of her chest rising and falling.

"Tell me what you are smelling, right now, as we speak."

"The starch in my dress, fresh from the cleaner's. Someone ate Chinese takeout in the lunchroom down the hall—yesterday. Three sprigs of lavender from the farm of a friend."

"It doesn't take a 'nose' to be able to smell lavender."

"How many people can distinguish between *Lavendula angustifolia, intermedia* and *dentate*?"

At that, there was enough of a pause to give her a flicker of hope.

"It's unprecedented. I'm not making any promises. Give me some time to think it over."

He'll say anything to get off the phone.

"What was your last name, again?"

"St. Pierre. Sauvignon St. Pierre."

Twenty-five hundred miles away in his New York City brownstone, Lawrence Van Horne was trying to enjoy his cocktail hour—that is, if he could ever get the persistent woman off the phone. Frowning, he reached around his wineglass for the bottle of his favorite cabernet, turning it to read the label.

"As in, Domaine St. Pierre?"

"Yes. Xavier St. Pierre is my father."

Lawrence inserted his nose into his balloon-shaped glass, closed his eyes, and took three short whiffs. He drank, swishing to allow the ruby liquid to wash over his tongue, soft palate, and epiglottis.

"Let's see what we can do," he replied.

* * *

A half hour later, Savvy was gazing out her office window at all the pretty spring colors, wondering how much essential oil could be distilled out of Rathmell Ranch's entire lavender harvest, when her phone rang.

"Savvy? Don Smith. Everything looks fine on the Morales contract. You want me to fax it over?"

"What?" She spun her chair back around with a clatter, to face her desk.

"You want me to fax it, or do you want to stop by and pick it up?"

"The partners accepted the Moraleses' counteroffer?"

"Yeah."

Her heart skipped a beat. "Already?"

"The sooner we can close, the better. We need to tear everything out of there, raze the buildings, and put in rootstock by next spring."

Savvy was speechless.

"You there?"

She stood. "Uh, yeah. Fax it over."

"Will do. Take care. We'll talk soon about where to hold the closing and all."

"Yippee!" Savvy's squeal had one of the assistants popping her head around the doorframe with a disapproving yet curious look.

Who cared what she thought? "Great news! I just did my first real estate deal!"

Esteban was loading the market gear into the back of his truck to prepare for the coming weekend, when Savvy's Mercedes pulled up the lane.

He was in high spirits. Sunday's passing shower hadn't affected the lavender at all. And now here came his two-legged mermaid. He hadn't been expecting her today on her way home from work, but he'd take it.

Her mile-wide grin matched his, as she got out of her car and wobbled rapidly toward him on those heels that made her calf muscles clench so sexily.

"Esteban!" she called breathlessly. Then he saw the long paper in her hand. It looked like the contract Padre had signed yesterday. A little ice chip formed in his belly.

"They took it! They took your offer!" she called when she was still yards away.

No puede ser! The ice chip expanded into an iceberg, filling his whole being, freezing his feet to the earth.

"Can you believe it?" By the time she reached him, she was practically panting.

He still couldn't move.

"Look." She thrust the contract toward him.

He didn't need to read it again. Against his will, he took it from her hand. One glance at the scrawled signature of NTI's general partner was all he needed. He shoved it back at Savvy like a hot potato.

"That's your copy," she said. Gently she pushed his hand back.

He didn't want a copy. He took her hand with one of his and pressed the papers into it with the other. Then he picked up the crate containing Madre's market scales and produce bags and deposited it into the truck bed.

Savvy's smile faded. She looked down at the papers, then up at him. "You're upset."

He stopped and stared at her. "Upset? *Upset? Qué demonios! ¿Qué quieres que diga? Toda mi punto de cambiar la vida!"*

With a grunt, he hefted the big white market canopy into the truck bed—a job that usually required two men—while she stood and watched. The hand holding the contract drifted down to her side.

"I know. You're in shock. The *Plan Familiar*, and all that."

"You say it like it's nothing! My grandfather's dream, my uncle's and father's work is just . . . pfffft—gone!" He threw his arms up. "What am I going to tell Padre?"

Savvy licked her lips and forced calm into her voice. "It was his offer. He set the price. He had to have known there was a chance NTI would take it."

"What about Madre?" He gestured wildly toward their humble house, where a ruffled curtain fluttered out the window in the spring breeze. So what if it wasn't a mansion? It was theirs. "She's worked her whole life to make this . . . this cinder-block box a home! What's going to happen to it now?"

Savvy studied her shoes. When she looked up again, a tear rolled beneath the rim of her glasses. "I'm sorry," she said. "I'm really sorry. I feel like I'm caught in the middle, here. I'm the one who started this whole thing. I never meant to hurt anybody. You've got to believe that, Esteban. I was only doing my job."

She laid the papers on the edge of the truck bed, turned, and walked away.

He didn't even notice Padre behind him until he spoke.

"You don't have to translate to me what that was about."

Esteban hung his head.

He felt his father's hand squeeze his shoulder. "Don't blame yourself. She's right. I was the one who made the offer."

Esteban looked up sharply.

"That's right. I understood her," his father said. "Your old *padre's* smarter than you think. Come. Let's figure this out together before we go in and break the news to your mother."

Chapter 26

Wednesday, Esteban went to Mass.

Thursday, he got a haircut.

Friday, the utility company told Esteban he could start anytime. He picked the day after the closing on his family's property. That way, he could spend the next thirty days helping his parents prepare to auction off the farm equipment and pack up the house.

Friday night, Madre invited Savvy to dinner.

"Come in, come in," said Mrs. Morales, pulling Savvy into her warm embrace.

"Is that a new dress?" asked Savvy, handing her a bottle of wine.

"Yes." She spun around. "You like?"

"It's lovely."

The dress wasn't the only change Savvy noticed. Esteban leaned against a doorframe with arms folded, watching her. He was rocking a hot new haircut. If he'd reminded her of the David before, now he was the spitting image of him, with those waves molding to his head. It was all she could do not to fly to him and run her fingers through the layers, but the two of them stood on shaky ground, despite a couple of brief phone calls over the past few days. In the first one, he'd apologized for overreacting—his term—to the sale of the property.

She'd been apprehensive about coming to dinner—she, the rich-girl troublemaker who lived in the mansion next door. So far, nobody had jumped down her throat. In fact, his mother actually seemed to be in a festive mood.

"So many changes since you were at our table last, eh?" Mrs. Morales smiled, motioning proudly toward the dining table. Pretty lace placemats dressed up the colorful stoneware. And tonight, instead of Coke, a bottle of Dos Equis sat above each plate. "Come. Sit."

"Yes, so many," Savvy said. She held out her plate while Mrs. Morales scooped enough enchiladas for three people onto it. "Whoa," she said, too late. Oh well. You had to pick your battles.

"What do you think of Esteban's haircut?"

She chanced a shy grin his way. "Very . . . hip." She'd opted for a ponytail again tonight, herself, after Esteban had complimented her on it during their picnic.

"Tomorrow is the market's opening day. And next week, Mr. Morales and I have an appointment with a Realtor to see some houses in Verdant Acres."

Really. Verdant Acres was a new over-fifty-five development on the other side of 29. Mrs. Morales sure hadn't wasted any time since the sales agreement had been signed. She sighed and fidgeted with the napkin in her lap. "They don't allow chickens there. I'll miss my girls, but . . ."

Oh, God. Was that a tear in her eye?

". . . I have to look at the bright side of things, right?"

Guilt stabbed at Savvy.

"You're still doing the farmers' market, then?"

"Only tomorrow. Why not? It's all ready to go. The equipment is packed. The stall rent is paid for the whole summer. It's a good way to see my friends, tell them the news, and sell what produce we can before . . ." Her mouth forced a tight smile.

Mr. Morales seemed as hard to read as ever. Did he hold the sale against Savvy? Blame her for derailing the *Plan Familiar*? Suddenly, her heart squeezed with empathy for the gruff immigrant. It must be hard to be left out of every conversation in which English was the primary language.

"Mr. Morales?" she said. *"Como estas?"*

He stopped chewing and raised suspicious eyes from his plate. After a pause, he replied, *"Estoy bien."*

"Espero que disfrutes esta próxima etapa de tu vida," said Savvy.

Mrs. Morales's smile grew and grew. She patted her husband's forearm, resting on the table. "Do you hear that? Savvy wishes you happiness in your new life. Isn't that nice."

He grunted.

Savvy shrugged. "Don't be too impressed. It's the only thing I know how to say in Spanish."

"You learned it just for him," his wife replied. A look of pure appreciation shone from her eyes.

Esteban went to the fridge and pulled out another Dos Equis. Savvy slid her untouched bottle toward Esteban's father's plate when she saw that his was low, and poured herself a scant glass of the cabernet she'd brought to show she still wanted to be part of the family's little celebration.

Later, when Madre had stepped out of the kitchen and Savvy was drying the last dish, she asked Esteban, "Want to go to Bodega for a nightcap? I'll drive."

At the bar, Esteban pounded yet another beer, while Savvy stuck with lemon water.

Next to them, a fortyish couple debated the details of their upcoming vacation as if it were a federal case. The woman sported inch-long, squared-off fingernails with white-painted tips. Her husband wore one of those color-blocked, silk bowling shirts.

"I say Florence. The art is better in Florence," declared French Nails.

"Your mother is so gracious. It felt wonderful to be invited to your house tonight," said Savvy. "I really think a lot of your family, you know."

"It's no secret Madre likes you."

"I can't help being a little worried, though."

"You're worried *now*? Now that it's a done deal?"

"Yes, I am." Before, the Moraleses had been just the faceless farmers next door. Jeanne raved about them now and then, and Papa ranted. Now they were real people. "How do you think this is going to shake out for your family? It's going to be a big change for them."

Esteban took another pull on his beer.

"I vote Rome," argued Bowling Shirt. "We can fly into Rome, get a car and maybe rent a villa in Tuscany, then circle back through Umbria. Maybe take a day trip to Sardinia."

"Seems like Madre's almost looking forward to moving," said Esteban sheepishly.

"Are you sure? Because to me it looked like maybe she was only pretending to be excited."

"Well, she did make that appointment to see that new housing development."

Savvy twirled her glass thoughtfully. "I hope she'll be happy."

"Don't worry about Madre. She's the backbone of the family. She'll be fine."

"What about your dad? I'm trying as hard as I can with him."

Esteban shook his head. "It's not you."

"Then what is it?"

"It's your father. He's tried to buy our land before. At first, when you brought us this latest offer, Padre thought it was just another of his ploys. That he was using you to go through me."

Savvy's hand flew to her heart. "Papa tried to buy your land? When? What happened?"

"Couple years ago. The same way as this time, a Realtor brought Padre an offer from a partnership. You know how our fathers feel about each other. They'd cross the street to avoid shaking hands. It didn't get too far before Padre said *nada*, no way."

French Nails argued, "You got to decide last time. It's my turn. I vote Florence. Suzie went there last year and she loved it. That's where she got her Fendi coat."

"I swear to you, Esteban, Papa has nothing to do with this."

"That's what I told Padre, but he doesn't trust any of the big vintners. He's afraid pretty soon all the land is going to be owned by anonymous corporations."

"I know land is being bought up by foreign companies. My father doesn't like that any more than yours does. They both believe the people making the decisions that affect local policy should be people who actually live here."

Esteban raised a brow. "You asked."

Time to change the subject.

"I called Anne Rathmell today. She said I could come back up and look at the still again Saturday morning, before I stop by the farmers' market to see your family's stall. I think I'm going to make her an offer on it. She's never even used it, so I can't imagine she'll say no."

"Where are you going to put it, now that I won't have a green-house anymore?"

"I guess I'll find a place in one of our outbuildings. It won't take up that much space."

"You ought to consider setting up a real distillery if you're plan-ning to start processing oil this summer."

"Did I tell you? That guy in New York is putting together a kit to see if I have the potential to be a real nose."

He peeled the label on his beer. "That's great, Savvy."

Her dream was growing while his was dying. Her heart ached for him. But letting on would only make things worse. Better to be en-couraging.

"Are you going to look for land somewhere else? Since you're not interested in grape growing, you won't have to limit yourself to the Valley. Judging by Rathmell Ranch, the poorer the soil, the better lavender likes it. You might be able to get something at a good price."

"With what?"

"The proceeds from the sale, of course."

He shook his head. "I'm not taking any of the proceeds."

"What? Surely your parents will want you to share in it."

"They offered. I turned them down."

"That's crazy."

"Why? It's not my money. I haven't done anything to deserve it."

"Are you kidding? You told me yourself, you've been working that farm since you were a little boy!"

"Yeah, helping Padre. He mapped out every bed. It was his farm. Everything was his idea."

She frowned.

"Granted, now my parents will have a decent nest egg. But they could live another thirty years. You know how expensive everything is. Mortgages, medicine. After they buy a house, they're going to need to invest the rest of the money. That's all they have to live on."

"That Spanish expression that you used right after I told you that NTI had accepted the counteroffer. What was that again?"

He lifted a hand and let it drop onto the bar. "Give me a hint. I was pretty whipsawed at the time."

"It sounded something like *cambiar la vida*."

"Oh, that. 'My whole life's about to change.' "

"So if you're not going to look for another place to grow lavender, then what are you planning to do?"

"I don't know," said French manicure. "Maybe we should just cruise the Rhine, instead."

"Let's get out of here," Esteban said, downing the rest of his beer.

Chapter 27

"Where are we going?" Savvy asked.

"Head south."

Down the road a bit, Esteban said, "One good thing that's coming out of this, I'm finally going to have my own place."

They both knew what that meant: *privacy.* But Savvy was still subdued.

"See that school up here on the right? Pull in behind it. Park in the back where there aren't any security lights, facing outward."

She did as he asked.

"Shut her off." In the dark, he saw her head turn toward him, wondering what they were doing there.

"This way we'll be sure to see any paparazzi that may have followed us."

There was nothing else to do then but come out with it. "Got a job with the utility company."

"Excuse me?"

"Going to be a lineman."

"The guy who climbs up the telephone poles and handles the high-voltage lines?"

In answer to his nod, she sat there speechless.

"What about your lavender?" she said after she recovered. "You had your heart set on that!"

"I told you, that dream's dead."

Through the gloom, he felt her glaring at him.

His hands went palms up in his lap. "I have nothing anymore, Savvy. I'm not like those people at the bar. The one percent, whose biggest decision is where to take their next vacation. I've got real world problems. Paying rent. Making sure my aging parents are set up."

"Your parents are going to be fine," she soothed. "Two million dollars is more money than they could ever have hoped to earn on that little farm. I can't understand why you don't want to keep pursuing your goal."

"That goal went hand in hand with carrying on the family tradition. I'm not sure one exists separate from the other." He scrubbed a hand through his cropped hair, still not used to what the barber had said was the latest style.

"Besides, I'd have to start all over. How long 'til I would turn a profit? I need to start making money right now.

"When do you start your new job?"

"Right after closing. 'Til then, it's going to be insane, what with looking for new places to live for my parents and myself, figuring out what goes and what gets tossed or auctioned off, and so on."

"Whatever happened to putting your hands in the dirt? Watching the seasons change? Being your own boss?"

"Maybe I'm not meant to be a farmer after all. It is kind of ironic, though. Just when those plants were starting to take hold . . ."

He looked down at his arm, where Savvy had laid her hand. "Don't pity me, Savvy. Don't ever pity me."

"Esteban! I'd never—"

He held up a halting hand. "Just listen." His beer buzz was coming in handy to say what he needed to say next.

"You see this parking lot? This used to be the place to go. For me and everyone else at Vintage High. I won't tell you how many times I've parked here, with how many girls. They mean nothing to me. After you, there's nobody. And I'm not talking about your money, this fancy car"—his eyes flitted around the dim interior, the rich upholstery, the expanse of fine wood trim—"or that big white house you grew up in."

She looked away, embarrassed. Because that was Savvy. She was more interested in meeting people, pursuing goals, discovering new things, than she was in money.

"And it's not because you look like a mermaid with glasses, either."

He heard a sniff, and he couldn't tell if it was a muffled laugh or she was crying.

"It's because I love your heart, and your energy, and your curious mind. You have this craving to learn about everything . . . nature, people, business . . . nothing's not interesting to you. You were even interested in my lame attempts to grow lavender. Do you know who else cared about that, over my whole lifetime? No one. Well, maybe Madre. Mothers are supposed to care about their sons.

"You know what else I love about you? That can-do attitude. I'll admit, it doesn't hurt that a, you have money—shut up, let me finish—and b, brains. There's nothing you can do about that. Those are things you were born with. Money opens doors, and so do smarts. But lots of rich, smart people aren't as positive, as engaged with the world as you. When you want something, you just go for it and assume you'll get it, and I have a feeling that usually, you do. You're so confident and self-assured. Want an example? Soon as I showed you a few varieties of lavender, you were off and running, calling up people to pick their brains, visiting that ranch. Now you're studying how to make perfume. You're amazing. Rich or poor, that's the kind of woman I want to spend the rest of my life with."

Now she was crying, for sure. Softly snuffling, not blubbering in a way that made him uncomfortable. But he wasn't through yet.

"Here's the thing, Savvy. Here's the thing. I don't have all those degrees, like you do. And I don't have a last name that opens doors. Up until yesterday, I thought that maybe—just maybe—there was an outside chance I could make something out of my experiments. Take what was handed down to me and become an entrepreneur, like your father. Become worthy of you in my own right. Now, all that's gone. I'm not ashamed of being a laborer, but I need to put it right out there, not hide from it. I know there's not a chance in hell you ever thought you'd end up with a common workingman. But if you'll have me, I'll make you the happiest damn woman on the planet. And that's a promise."

"Oh, Esteban." Savvy leaned past the steering wheel to put her arms around his neck. "You already have."

Her cheek was wet. She dipped her head to kiss him, and he took it up a notch, delving into her mouth with his tongue, reaching to cup her dainty breast, loving how his outsized hand dwarfed it even more.

Her fingers slid between the snaps on his shirt.

He took a steadying breath. "You don't know what that does to me."

Her hand left his chest to curl around his quad, where his thigh met his torso.

"Savvy." She was ten inches shorter than he and a hundred and thirty pounds lighter. So how was it that she could control him with a feather-light touch of her fingertips?

He removed her hand from his thigh, kissed it, and held it to his chest. "Not in the car. You're too good for that. Give me a week, and I'll have a place for us to go to be alone together. *Cristo*, give me 'til tomorrow."

Pop, pop, pop went his shirt snaps, and she bowed to nuzzle his chest with her nose.

He closed his eyes and rested his head against the leather headrest, picturing them as they had been the day they'd met, she in her tight-ass bun and nun's habit, he grungy as a stray dog.

Who would've believed that, two months later, he'd be stroking the length of her long, thick locks as she kissed a path down his stomach?

Gently, firmly, he pulled her up. "Hey. We took one chance already."

In the past, any other woman would have had to hold him back like a freight train. But with Savvy everything was different. He exalted her. And hopefully, this was only the beginning. They had a lifetime ahead of them to do things right.

"Wait." She reached into the back seat and found her bag. Rummaging around, she pulled out—not a foil square, as he'd expected—but a tumble of small boxes. "Look what I have," she sang like a teenager, spilling them onto his lap.

"What the—?" he exclaimed. "What is this, Christmas? What are we going to do with all these?"

"Use them, what else?" she answered. There was just enough moonlight to catch the glint in her eyes. Until him, she'd been a twenty-seven-year-old virgin. She was so, so late to the party. So sophisticated, and yet so naïve.

He rifled through the boxes, straining to pick out the descriptive lettering on them. "What'd you do, buy one of everything?" He couldn't help chuckling at her zeal to catch up.

"Well," she said defensively, "I wasn't sure what size you were, what kind you liked."

"You weren't sure what size I was?" His laughter came harder.

"I have no one to compare you to," she huffed.

"Oh, my." Now he was having trouble breathing, he was laughing so hard. "You see? This is what I'm talking about. Everything you do, you go all the way."

Savvy wasn't laughing, though. She'd begun gathering up all the boxes from the seat and where they'd spilled onto the floor, shoving them back into her bag.

"What's the matter?" he asked, wiping tears of laughter from his eyes. "What are you doing?"

"I'm putting them away. Sorry for not being a prophylactic pro."

"Hold it." He reached for her. "Did I hurt your feelings?"

Her jerking her arm away was answer enough.

"*Chula*, the first time, I was out of my mind. That was a . . . a celebration of being alive." He wanted every time they made love to be a celebration. He didn't want anything coming between them. Not even a sheath of latex.

But he also didn't want her to ever have to look back and wonder if a poor boy had trapped a rich girl into marrying him by getting her pregnant. He wanted her to say yes of her own free will, not out of any obligation.

While she was still rounding up her stupid boxes, he got out of the car, strode around to her side, and yanked open her door, holding out his hand. "Don't worry about those. Come here."

She still looked hurt, though she didn't object when he reached for her hand and gently tugged. Just tumbled out and leaned against the car with her arms folded.

"There's more than one way to get the job done, counselor," he whispered. He reached up and took off those infernal glasses, laying them on the roof. Then he began gently working out the elastic band that held back her glossy auburn mane. Finally the band sprang away into oblivion. Then he lowered his head to hers.

She was slow to respond. But when he pulled her to him and kissed her, his hand making circles on the small of her back, her mouth parted . . . a little. And then, eventually, her arms unfolded and found their way around his neck.

Esteban flipped up her skirt and slid his fingers up her leg to her hip, then under the side of her panties. Felt like lace this time. *Sweet.* Not that it mattered. She would be hot even in burlap. Then he switched hands, working the thin, stretchy material down first one side and then the other until they finally dropped.

He slid his hands under her ass and easily scooped her up, leaving her white panties lying in a heap on the black pavement. Inexperienced as she was, her legs somehow instinctively knew how to wrap themselves around his waist, locking at the ankle.

Now she was right where he wanted her, sandwiched between him and the Mercedes, suspended by a combination of the tilt of her pelvis, the slope of the car, and his hips. The heat of her body activated her fragrance. They kissed in the ways they'd already discovered, and added more.

They were in a public area. Anyone—the cops, the paparazzi—could pull in at any time. But they were still fully clothed. If he saw headlights, it would only be a matter of smoothing down Savvy's dress.

He couldn't see it in the dark—couldn't even feel it through his coarse pants, but he knew that her most sensitive, intimate place pressed, vulnerable and open, against the rough denim of his jeans, and it made him almost *loco* with desire to please her. He began rocking against her, slowly at first, then faster as her body responded. Her grip on his neck grew tighter. Behind their kisses, she started making little mewling noises in her throat. When she had to tear her lips from his or suffocate, he peered down on her face in the moonlight and watched her lose control, panting as he kept up the rhythm.

Chula.

When she collapsed against him like a rag doll, he felt like the king of the world. He stayed with her, cupping her rear . . . biding his time until her shredded breaths tapered off to sighs.

After reining himself in to focus on her pleasure, her total innocence of his plan for what he intended to do to her next was almost too much for him to endure.

When she finally found the strength to lift her head off his shoulder, thinking they were finished, he stroked the hair away from her damp temple and kissed her forehead. Savvy moistened her dry lips with the tip of her tongue and smiled.

That's when he knew it was time.

Slipping his hand between them, he found the slickness he'd known would be there, and used it to ease the friction.

The pleasure it gave him to surprise her with another orgasm so quickly more than made up for containing his own.

"*Mía*." he whispered in her ear. *Mine.*

Chapter 28

Opening day. The day his family worked toward all year long. Madre always arranged their harvest in a way that made the Moraleses' stall look more colorful, more luscious than everyone else's. She chatted with the women, exclaiming over their cell phone photos of their growing children, and upsold the men with their meager grocery lists. Once people tasted the Moraleses' tasty products, they almost always came back for more.

Esteban pitched in wherever he was needed, loading and unloading the crates of produce, helping sell when Madre got too busy, emptying the cashbox into the bank pouch when the stack of ones started spilling over, same as he always did.

This year's opening day felt different, though, thanks to the GOING OUT OF BUSINESS sign that Esteban had scribbled and stuck in the ground. The news quickly spread that the Moraleses' first market Saturday of the year would also be their last. Madre still smiled for the customers and Padre still hung out quietly in the background, but Esteban knew that deep down inside, they harbored the same confused feelings he did.

He had to admit, from a purely practical standpoint, Savvy was right. It made sense to take the two million and walk away. No more money worries, no more aching backs. Still, this market was a part of them. They were saying good-bye to a whole way of life.

Just like Bodega, the market was a melting pot of Napa Valley. Its packed stalls were a feast for the eyes as well as the palate. Especially on opening day, it was hard not to run into someone you knew. Esteban was toting another case of bags from the truck about mid-morning when he spotted Shane, sauntering shoulder to shoulder through the alley with a gang of guys from downtown. One of the guys, Justin

Thompson, was okay, but most of the others were the type who bounced from job to job, earning just enough to get wasted most nights. If it weren't for the free live music and festival atmosphere of opening day, they probably wouldn't be at the market.

"Hey, E!"

Esteban nodded, his face half hidden behind the large box in his arms. From the corner of his eye, he saw Shane elbow the biggest man—Steve something, his name was. Years back, Steve had given Esteban the stink eye at a bar over a girl they both were hitting on. A girl so insignificant Esteban couldn't even recall her face.

"Dude. What happened to your hair?" prodded Steve with a cocky grin.

Let it slide.

"Oh, yeah, thanks a lot for dumping me at Salt Point a couple weeks ago," said Shane, throwing up gang signs with his hands.

What Esteban wanted to say was how ballsy the slightly built Shane was when he was surrounded by a pack of thugs. But he had better things to do.

"Thinks he's better than everyone else since he's humping one of the St. Pierre sisters," called out Shane to his back.

He felt his jaw set. Let them have their fun. They weren't worth the trouble of wiping blood off his knuckles. But he couldn't resist a glance.

"What?" Shane spread his arms innocently, walking backward, his eyes flickering left and right for moral support. "Everyone's talking about it. They're all like, what's *he* doing with *her?* And I'm like, happens all the time. Everybody knows those wine princesses love to go slumming. Hook up with the help."

Esteban kept on walking, his temples beginning to throb with his blood pressure.

"You seen her? The brunette one with the glasses? I'd tap that," said an unfamiliar voice.

"You know how it goes," said Shane, raising his voice even louder so Esteban would be sure to hear. "It never lasts."

Esteban was almost to the stand when he heard their parting comment.

"Gonna be a kept man, now that ol' Xavier St. Pierre bought out the Moraleses, lock, stock, and barrel."

He stopped in his tracks then. Set down the box. Turned. The others were now hastening away with wary backward glances.

Not Shane. Printed boxers bagging above the waistband of his jeans, still counting on the half dozen larger men to stand up for him, he continued to taunt.

"Didn't know that, huh? Look at him. He looks so surprised. It's a bitch when you're the last one to know, isn't it, E?"

How he got there, he'd never know, but Esteban found himself on top of the smaller man, fist poised above his face. "That's where it ends," he growled.

Shane covered his face with his hands. "Hide your crazy, man! Don't blame me—ask Hector! That's who told me!"

Hector, Shane's cousin. A wine distributor.

"Everyone knows. Tell him." From where Esteban was trying not to bash his face into the pavement, Shane's neck craned behind him to his gang, who had stopped some feet way. Too brave to run, not brave enough to enter the fray.

Esteban peered up at them too, searching face after face, the question plain in his eyes.

"It's true, man," Justin Thompson said, his voice holding a twinge of regret. Justin's mom had worked in a winery since before God was born. She knew everybody and everybody knew her.

Esteban let go of Shane, rose and stood over him, unseeing. There was one way to find out for sure. When Savvy got there, she'd refute what they'd said. *She would.*

Shane scrambled to his feet and strode away brushing the dirt off his sleeves, cocky as ever.

Esteban turned to see Padre standing white-faced at the rear of their market stand. Sweat beaded on his forehead.

"Padre?"

He ran to him.

"Padre?"

Chapter 29

Finally, the weekend! Savvy stretched, yawned, and picked up her phone on the bedside table to check the time. Today was going to be a busy one. She planned to be at the ranch to look at the still by nine-thirty, then hit the market during its peak hours.

Her emotions zig-zagged as she went through her morning routine. She was excited to visit the Rathmell Ranch again and finally experience the market Jeanne had been raving about all these years. But she couldn't shake her guilt. Her first market visit would be the Moraleses' last day in business.

Selling still made sense from a money standpoint, but the major lifestyle change was going to take the Moraleses some getting used to. Normally, retiring and selling a home was something people took years to map out. By the time they finally made a decision, they'd already worked through some of the feelings of loss and resignation that came with the freedom of letting go.

If only retiring had been the Moraleses' idea. If only Savvy hadn't been the one to impose it on them.

While she waited for Anne Rathmell to answer her knock, Savvy studied the alcove surrounding the entrance to the ranch house. It could use a little attention. Clearly, the leggy weeds springing up around the squat silver and gray succulents weren't part of the original landscape design.

The door swung wide, but it wasn't Anne on the other side. Savvy lowered her gaze to a man in a paint-spattered cotton smock, seated in a wheel chair.

"Hi. I'm Savvy. I think Anne is expecting me?"

"Lucas Rathmell. Watch it—I seem to get paint everywhere when I work," he warned before shaking her hand.

Savvy smiled. "Don't worry. One of my sisters is an artist."

He wheeled himself around to go down the extra-wide hallway, and Savvy noticed even his chair was smudged with blotches of color.

"Annie?" Lucas called out. "Someone here to see you."

Anne appeared from around a corner, slightly breathless. "Didn't hear the bell. I was on the computer doing one of those—what do you call it? Video-chatting things—with an old colleague from Stanford. Sorry to interrupt your painting, Lucas."

"S'okay. Needed to stretch my legs, anyway." He grinned at being the butt of his own joke.

"Did you two meet? Hold on, Savvy, let me find my sun hat."

On their way to the distillery, Anne asked, "Just you today?"

"Esteban's family runs a stall at the Napa farmers' market. Today's their opening day. I'm going down as soon as I leave here." Thinking about seeing him made her heart flutter.

Anne looked at her. "I was going to ask if the two of you are close, but that look in your eyes says it all. He's not what he seems on the surface, you know."

Savvy shot her a curious look. "What do you mean?"

"He may look like nothing but a big, strapping farm boy," said Anne, holding open the distillery door for her. "But there's a lot going on up here." She tapped her head. "He's very bright. And very sensitive. Don't forget, I was a clinical psychologist for many years. I'm pretty good at reading people."

Inside the distillery, a decade's worth of dust bombarded Savvy's nose. She sneezed.

"It's a disaster in here, isn't it?" said Anne.

More dust motes stirred up by their boots clouded the air, filtered by rays of pale light that managed to get through a grimy skylight. Built-in shelves lined the room, no doubt designed for holding the yield from the still.

Savvy walked over to the machine and drew a visible line in the soot along its girth, wondering if the brown tarnish could ever be rubbed off the copper. In her mind's eye, she saw the sun glinting orange off the still's newly restored finish, the shelves filled with sparkling glass bottles. "Oh, no, it's great." She spread her arms and spun around. "I'm in love with it. All of it."

Savvy was glad Anne thought it was a wreck. That meant she'd be more likely to let it go.

"What would you say if I offered to take it off your hands?" she asked.

"What? You want to buy that old thing?"

At that moment, Savvy couldn't imagine anything she'd like more than fixing up that still, stuffing its canister full of lavender, and sniffing the heavenly scented hydrosol and essential oil that came out the other end.

"What on earth would you do with it? Where would you put it?"

"I could find a place at my family's winery."

"Aren't you all tied up being a lawyer?"

There was that. Interesting. She never felt this enthusiastic sitting at her desk at Witmer, Robinson and Scott.

Slowly, she traversed the room's corners, imagining how she would transform it if it were hers. A table over *here*, cupboards for lab equipment over *there* . . .

"Hmmm?"

"You haven't heard a thing I've said."

Savvy pulled a face. "Sorry! Just thinking."

"You're quite serious about this, aren't you?"

"We'll see." She shrugged. "I've been told I have a 'nose.' "

"Tell you what. You can have the still. Do anything you want with it. Why not keep it here? Easier than you and me taking it apart and hauling it out to your car, getting ourselves and your seats all dirty. Lord knows, there's a ton of raw material to work with here. More than one person could ever process."

Savvy's eyes threatened to bulge out of their sockets. "Are you serious?"

Anne's eyebrows went up under the brim of her hat. "Like I said earlier, Lucas and I didn't move here for the lavender.

"Besides, I'm going to be traveling a lot this summer. The project I was telling you about? I'm collaborating on another book—that's who I was online with when you came."

"*Another* book?" Savvy asked, impressed.

Anne waved away Savvy's admiration. "Nothing you'd be interested in. Merely a dry, clinical piece about personalities. That's my area of expertise. Now, I know what you're thinking—these things can all be done on the computer nowadays—but there's something to be said for a good, old-fashioned meeting in the flesh. Spreading out all your papers, comparing notes. I've taken an apartment on the Stanford campus, to be closer to my writing partner for a few days out of the week.

"So why don't you simply come up here and work, whenever the spirit moves you? Easier than dismantling this old thing and lugging it down to where you'll also have to transport raw material, anyway."

"What about your husband?"

"What about him?"

"He won't mind me poking around the property?"

"Pfft. Lucas won't even notice you're here. He's getting ready for a show. Totally self-sufficient, holed up in his studio. Painting was always *his* dream . . . though I can't imagine why we thought we had to live all the way out here in Timbuktu to write and paint. Could have stayed in Cupertino, where the sun shines two hundred sixty-five days a year, all the sidewalks have curb cuts to accommodate his chair, and there's a decent restaurant on every corner."

"He seems happy enough," Savvy said.

"Hmph. Usually. Last winter got to him a little."

"How does this sound?" asked Savvy. "Let me give you some money for the still. At least a token amount—before you see how nice it looks when I polish it up and you change your mind," she ribbed, "and I'll take you up on your offer to keep it here, until I think of something better."

Anne thrust out her hand. "Deal. If you ever come to your senses, feel free to either take it with you or simply walk away, no harm done."

Waving a hand in front of her face, Anne headed for the door. "This dust is killing me. Poke around here as long as you like. I have research to do." She took another step, then halted. "And Savvy, there's something else. I feel I owe you an apology," she said from the doorway.

"What on earth for?"

"The first time you called me on the phone? When you said you were one of the St. Pierres, I was expecting this pampered heiress . . . a self-centered socialite. Just look at you, though . . ."

Savvy's hand automatically flew to the elastic band she'd hastily stretched through her hair, lowering her gaze to the roomy flowered cotton dress she'd borrowed from Char, all the way down to her rubber boots. She must look a fright.

"Grounded as they come. And me, with my doctorate and all my books . . ." She exited, chiding herself as she walked away. "You'd think I'd know better than to believe in stereotypes. . . ."

As Savvy wove through the crowd of shoppers at the farmers' market, listening to the vendors hawking their wares—"Here, try a piece of our Taleggio. It's a semi-soft, washed-rind cheese"—admiring the stalls with their artfully staged breads and pyramids of free-range eggs and, of course, fruits and veggies. The sun warming her back made dancing shadows of the pedestrian's legs on the macadam. Best of all, she'd just bought her very own copper still! Her heart felt ready to burst with well-being.

While Savvy imagined the scent of her personal blends of essential oils, the actual aromas of the market—sweet, yeasty, pungent—swirled along on the air currents like tangible things.

And all the while, snippets of last night kept coming back to her, each one inciting a secret smile. Esteban, kissing her in ways she'd never even imagined only a few weeks ago. Those panties she'd agonized over at the department store, discarded like a candy bar wrapper. The way his touch had made her feel as if she were endlessly freefalling, only to find herself landing safely in his strong arms. . . .

Bump!

Something knocked Savvy out of her reverie. A small boy raced by, dipping and dodging between the shoppers.

"Sorry!"

The exuberance on his freckled face instantly replaced her annoyance with a smile. Another scamp whizzed after the first one in a merry chase. Within seconds, both kids had disappeared into the throng, leaving Savvy more thrown off at the sight of her hand lying protectively across her tummy than at having been jostled.

The distillery and the market weren't the only reasons today was such a big day for Savvy. This day marked two months since she'd bled.

One trip to the pharmacy and she'd know for sure. So why hadn't she taken the test?

At first, she'd put it off because she was afraid it would come back positive. But as the days and weeks went by, something in her heart grew along with her belly. It had started out as acceptance, and turned into hope. Now, she was scared to take that test for fear it would come out negative.

There it was, the sign heralding MORALES FARM.

Strangely, with all those people milling about, the stall was unmanned. Savvy stood in front of it, her brow furrowed. Where was Mrs. Morales? Where were Esteban and his father? It was a busy time for them all to be taking a break. They were apt to miss some good sales.

The pie vendor at the counter next to the Moraleses' called over to her. "If you want to buy something from their stall, I can help you."

Savvy drifted over and waited until the customer in front of her paid for her pies.

"Where are the Moraleses?" asked Savvy.

"They took Mr. Morales to Queen of the Valley in an ambulance. Mrs. Morales rode along. I told her I'd keep an eye out for her customers, close up for her at the end of the day if she's not back . . ."

Savvy had pulled her phone out of her bag before she even realized it and was punching in Esteban's number.

It rang and rang.

She started sprinting back in the direction from which she'd come. Now every pedestrian was just an obstacle in her path.

When she got to her car, she threw her phone onto the passenger seat unanswered, and headed toward the hospital.

Chapter 30

The sharp odor of disinfectant burned in Savvy's throat. She glanced around at the people sitting calmly throughout the lobby, amazed that she was the only one who seemed to be affected.

She found Mrs. Morales perched on the edge of a vinyl seat in the waiting room of the ER, shredding a tissue.

Breathlessly, Savvy sat down beside her and took her outstretched hand. "How is your husband?"

"They still do the tests," she said.

Savvy searched her face for more.

"It's his heart."

"Oh, no."

Mrs. Morales stifled a sob. "It's that old feud between Geraldo and your papa."

Savvy angled her head. "What?" With a sinking feeling, she half rose, skimming the room. "Where's Esteban?"

"He—Esteban is very angry."

She was confused. Angry? Because his father had a heart attack? "What happened?"

"He—" She bent her head and held her tissue to her nose until she composed herself. "I don't know how to tell you this. He heard a rumor that your papa is the one who buys our property."

"That's not true! Who told him that?"

"I don't know. Some boys at the market. Troublemakers. It doesn't matter."

"Where is he?"

"He went outside to get some air, calm down."

"Which way?"

The sadness on Mrs. Morales's face gave way to apprehension. "Maybe you should wait a little . . ."

"Which way?"

Reluctantly, she pointed toward a door with her chin.

A carbon copy of the David was easy to spot, even in a parking lot the size of the hospital's. Savvy joggled up to him and put a hand on his arm. "Esteban. Tell me what happened."

He stopped pacing and gave her a look she'd never forget.

"How about *you* tell *me* what happened," he ground out. "The truth, this time."

"I don't know what you heard, but Papa had nothing to do with buying your land. You saw the agreement. . . ."

"I saw Napa Terroir Investments. I saw the name Don Smith. What I didn't see—what was kept *hidden* from me and my father—was the name Xavier St. Pierre!"

Savvy shook her head. "No," she whispered.

"You aren't the only one with connections, you know!" He jerked his arm away. "I have friends in this valley, too."

She wanted to ask who'd been feeding him his information, but a budding dread told her it didn't matter. Something her boss had said when he'd assigned her this case came back to her.

"One of the partners is an old friend of mine. We'll work it so that you get a nice commission."

Papa.

Esteban's pacing skidded to a halt. "You lied to me. Made fools out of me and my family, in front of the whole town. Faked an interest in my diving, my lavender, suckered me into selling our family home, just so you could pass your first—big . . ." He hunted for the right words. *"Career test!"* he spat out finally.

He closed the space between them until his face towered over her. Never had he looked larger than he did at that moment.

"Let me tell you something. I never once drew my fist at a man, until you came into my life."

Savvy could almost feel the heat from the fire in his eyes.

"In the past two weeks I almost decked *two* men." He leaned in even further, forcing her head backward. "Are you that good, or am I that stupid?"

She had to make him understand. "Esteban, I never—"

"You never cared for me! It's true what they say about the St. Pierres. They'll do anything—step on anyone—to get what they want.

"Do you know how hard it was for me to tell you about Padre's counteroffer? About wanting to turn our property into a lavender farm, when everyone else was scoffing at my idea? Our *Plan Familiar?*"

"I—I'm sorry—I wasn't—"

"You expect me to believe you weren't in on it? That you didn't know? You're a fucking *lawyer!*"

He whirled away, running his hand through his hair, then just as quickly whipped back around.

"You probably weren't even a virgin that day on the beach! *Mierda*—it wouldn't surprise me if you *faked* that blood! It was all just part of your scheme!"

His face was so close to hers now she could see the fleck of spittle clinging to the corner of his mouth.

The earth was spinning faster, faster, out of control.

Her own father had used her for his gain, destroying Esteban's love and respect for her in the process. Could no one, nothing, be depended on?

She'd heard of people's lives passing before their eyes. Now that was happening to her. Everything she thought she knew was wrong. Everything she'd spent her life doing was worthless.

Her powerlessness when Maman died and Papa divided her from her sisters . . . years (not to mention entire lines of letters on the Snellen eye chart) lost to mind-numbing study in her desperation to regain her self-confidence, a sense of control . . . ridiculous fantasies of developing her "nose" . . .

Past, present, and future swirled together, snaking and twisting their way down some vast vortex. The parking lot beneath her feet swayed, sending her hands spreading for balance. She hoped Esteban was too distracted to notice. She had to get out of there before she collapsed on the pavement. If anything could make this worse, it would be diverting to *her* the attention that belonged to Mr. Morales.

Esteban's mouth was moving again. She struggled to understand the words on his lips. "I want out of that sales agreement." He pointed at her for emphasis. "I'll hire my own lawyer and sue you to get out of it if I have to."

He started backing up, as if she were toxic. "And stay away from my family, you hear? You've already done enough damage—*counselor.*"

The world was disintegrating around her, leaving her lost... adrift. Somehow, she staggered back to her car.

Her hands knew what to do with the ignition button, to grasp the wheel at ten and two, but her mind spun like a pinwheel in a tornado. She forced deep breaths, trying to calm down enough to drive without getting in an accident, adding to her string of casualties.

Jeanne was at the front door wearing a concerned expression when Savvy arrived, alerted by the electronic tone that sounded whenever a car pulled onto the drive.

"Ah, mademoiselle, I have been talking to Maria."

Savvy burst out bawling. "Everything is so messed up." Her sobs echoed throughout the spacious marble foyer.

"I know. I know." Jeanne stroked Savvy's hair and let her weep.

"It's Papa again. Just when things were going so well, he has to screw everything up."

"Shhh..."

"And now"—*sniff*—"now Esteban thinks I was in on it the whole time.... He didn't believe me when I said I was as surprised as he was...." She wiped her eyes with her sleeve. "Where is everyone?" she hiccupped.

"Char went somewhere with Ryder. Meri is staying in the city for the weekend. It's only you and me."

"Where's Papa?"

"Did you forget? He went to Los Angeles."

With everything that had happened, she had forgotten. Papa often flew to L.A. during this slow time of year.

She clenched her jaw. "I need to talk to him."

After visiting the hospital early Sunday morning, Esteban accompanied Madre to Mass. While she knelt in prayer, Esteban sat on the stone-hard pew, gazing up at the stained-glass windows in the apse of St. Apollinaris. "Thank you for not letting him die," he prayed—just in case He'd had anything to do with it.

The doctor had confirmed what he already knew. The shock that Esteban had unwittingly sold their family farm to his worst enemy had triggered a severe spasm of Padre's right coronary artery. The good news was he didn't need surgery. The bad—his farming days were over. The less stress he had, mentally and physically, the longer he might live.

It seemed like a good sign when Padre had asked him to elevate the head of his bed earlier, when they'd entered his hospital room. Madre had guided the straw from his big Styrofoam cup of water to his mouth.

"How you doing, Papi?"

Lying there sucking obediently on his straw, he'd looked shockingly old. You could tell they had him all drugged up.

When Madre had forced as much liquid into him as he could take without bursting, he lay back on his pillow, licking his dry lips.

"Envidia."

"What's that, Papi?"

"Envidia," he rasped. "Those *matóns* at the market. They were jealous. Of you, with your high-class *chula*. Of all of us, for getting such a price for our land. Much more than it's worth."

Madre eyed Esteban uneasily.

"Are you saying I didn't *deserve* Savvy?"

"No!" said Madre, with a reassuring palm on Esteban's arm. "That's not what he means. Not what *envidia* means."

"Then what?"

Padre blinked and nodded to Madre, as if to say, *You tell him. I'm too tired.*

"Ahem." Madre cleared her throat and turned to Esteban. "How do I explain to you? It's not spoken of so much, here. . . . I haven't heard of it since we left the Michoacán."

She looked to Padre for the right words, but his eyes had closed. "It's not that *you* are evil when something unexpectedly good happens to you. It's when *certain people*—could be anyone—see that you have more than they do. They become jealous. Give you the evil eye, which in turn gives you bad luck. To balance the scales, so to speak."

Esteban turned to Papa, incredulous. "You think you had a heart attack because people envied you?"

Padre opened his eyes, but they had a faraway look. He seemed to be looking only within.

Esteban had already concluded Padre was on some heavy-duty

meds. He went to the bedside. "Don't worry, Papi. I'm going to get our land back."

"Now, now, let's not talk of that today," said Madre, fussing with the sheets, rearranging the things on his tray. "All your *padre* needs to think about now is getting better."

But Esteban *had* to think about it. If he didn't, who would?

Chapter 31

"You going to Mass?" Char's voice filtered through Savvy's closed bedroom door.

"No." She drew the covers up to her chin, and closed her eyes, wishing she could forget yesterday had ever happened. If she hadn't been able to sleep all night though, how could she now, with the sun streaming through her floor-to-ceiling windows?

She sighed, threw back the covers, splashed her face with cold water, and went downstairs. Knowing she'd find Jeanne at the breakfast table, surrounded by the papers, a tiny cup of espresso, and a large croissant, was something she looked forward to most Sunday mornings. Yet not even that comforted her this morning.

There Jeanne sat, as expected. Up at five, to early Mass, and back already.

"Come and sit down." She patted the seat next to her. "Let me look at you." Jeanne cupped Savvy's chin. "I know what you need."

Jeanne's coddling wasn't helping today. If Savvy were feeling better, she might have reached for the front page of the *Chronicle* to check out the headlines, even though she usually got her news online. Not today.

Behind her, Savvy heard the clink of china, the beep of the microwave.

Soon Jeanne was back with a mug of cocoa and a plate of—*shortbread?*

Savvy frowned, studying the flecks of purple in the shortbread. "What's that?"

"An old French remedy for women in your . . . who feel like you do this morning. An aide for the digestion."

Her stomach rumbled. Cautiously, she nibbled off a corner.

Jeanne picked up the paper where she'd left off. "No Mass today?"

Savvy shook her head. She managed to down a rectangle of shortbread and a few sips of cocoa before something on the back of the paper caught her eye: US DIVORCE RATE CLIMBS TO NEW HIGH.

"Did you happen to mention to Char that I want to talk to her about her prenup?" she asked halfheartedly.

Jeanne sipped her espresso. "Why are you concerned with your sister's life, mademoiselle, when you are so busy with problems of your own?"

Savvy looked up with determination. "I'll never be too busy for my sisters." Besides, thinking about Char's life was a welcome distraction this morning.

Jeanne slid on her readers to scrutinize some small type. "Very admirable. But just now, it seems that Chardonnay and Merlot have all of their—how do you say it? Ducks in a line."

"Row. Ducks in a row," said Savvy glumly. Shortbread dunked in cocoa was pretty good. Even better than Oreos and milk.

"You are the one who appears to be in need of some assistance."

Savvy ignored that. "So did you talk to her?"

Jeanne took off her readers, folded her arms on the table, and studied Savvy. "Have you spoken to Esteban since yesterday?"

Savvy shook her head. "He hates me." Though she'd thought there were no tears left in her, one surprised her by squeezing out, sliding down her cheek.

"Ah, *chére.*" Jeanne patted her hand. "Trust me. That man does not hate you."

"Yes, he does."

"*Au contraire.* In fact, I have never seen a man more in love than Esteban Morales. Why else does it pain him so much, to believe you are cognizant of what your papa does?"

Savvy's eyes went to Jeanne's. "Why is Papa like that?"

Jeanne slid out of her chair and went around the table to slide her arm around her. She stroked a hand down Savvy's hair, tucking it back over her shoulder. "Your papa, he is what is he is, and he does what he does. That, you will never change. The question is, what are *you* going to do?"

Savvy rubbed her sore eyes gently and sniffed. Jeanne drew a tissue from a box on the counter and put it in her hand.

"Thanks. I have an idea," she said, honking into the tissue.

"Aha. It's as I thought. You were always the smart one."

There were still details to be figured out. "I'm sorry. I know you mean well, but I'm not ready to talk about it."

"Of course, of course. Why be hasty? You have all the time in—" She caught her tongue. "Well"—she busied herself gathering up the newspapers into a neat pile—"you have *some* time. Enough, I'm sure, to conceive of a good plan."

Her hand hesitated over Savvy's empty plate. *"Fini?"*

Savvy looked up at her with gratitude. "Finished."

"Feel a little better now?"

She nodded, rose, and put her arms around Jeanne.

Jeanne took hold of Savvy's shoulders. "Listen to me. It is commendable to want to take care of your sisters, but they are grown women now, aren't they?"

"But—"

"They are not afraid to ask for your help when they need it. Hmm?"

Savvy stiffened. Looking out for her sisters had been her passion project since she was twelve. Nobody could tell her Char and Meri didn't need her. She had the evidence in their very own handwriting.

"Chardonnay should be the one to tell you this, not me. However, you know how she shies from any sort of controversy. Since she is having such trouble finding time to discuss it with you, I'm thinking perhaps she does not *want* a premarital agreement."

"What?"

"You have such strong feelings about this. Is it any surprise? You—our resident lawyer—whose own parents had a troubled relationship? Who doesn't even know what a healthy marriage looks like? And while we are all very proud of what you've accomplished, you have been so determined to protect your sisters, I think sometimes you cannot hear their opinions. You may not have accepted it yet, but soon, your sisters will be gone, starting their new lives with their husbands.

"It's time for you to concentrate on what *you* want, Sauvignon. What you *really* want—in your heart. Do you understand?"

After another quick squeeze, Jeanne released Savvy and went to the sink to wash up the breakfast dishes.

Back in her room, Savvy pulled out the yellowed letters she'd carried around in her bag for the past fourteen years.

She sat down on her bed and unfolded one of them.

Dear Savvy, How are you? I am fine. I hate it here. I don't have any friends. I miss you. I miss Char and my friends. I miss Jeanne and Papa. I can't wait to go home. Will you figure out a way we could all go back home again? Love, Merlot

Beneath the block printing was a sketch of three girls holding hands. Two brunettes and a blonde, lined up like Matryoshka dolls in descending order of height. The eyes were oversized and expressive, colored in with brown, green, and blue pencils. Meri had drawn big fat alligator tear rolling down the face of the shortest girl. At age eight, she was already expressing herself through art.

Tenderly, Savvy set the fragile paper aside.

Char's note was next.

TOP SECRET. Dear Savvy, Do you have a phone? We aren't supposed to use the one here in the hall, but everyone does anyways after Mrs. K goes to sleep. She'd written out the number. *Please, please call me. I miss you. Love, Chardonnay. P.S. Don't forget to call!*

Savvy sighed. The very day she'd received that letter, she'd forced herself to stay up 'til midnight, then tiptoed into her own hallway, letting the phone at Char's school ring and ring until an angry adult had answered.

"Who is this? Don't call this number! This phone is only for emergencies!" *Click.*

Apparently, the girls who successfully used the phone in Char's hallway were making *outgoing* calls, not receiving them. Poor Char hadn't thought that through.

The last letter was another one from Char.

Dear Savvy, Why don't you call me? I listen for the phone every night, but it never rings. Did you get my letter? I want to go home. This isn't like my old school. Please, do something. I miss you so much. Please call . . .

She refolded the letters along their fragile creases. Automatically, she started to return them to her purse, then stopped.

After all this time, whenever she imagined Char and Meri, she still saw those drawings of Matryoshka dolls in her mind.

She tried to picture her sisters as they were now, all grown up. Char with her children's foundation, engaged to a man whose drive to do good matched her own—a man who'd only started accepting acting gigs to support his family, after his father died. To meet Ryder, you'd never guess he was now one of the biggest actors in Hollywood.

And Meri, whose jewelry line was really taking off, thanks to her collaboration with the delicious Mark Newman. Talk about a match made in heaven.

Maybe Jeanne was right. Maybe her sisters were doing fine . . . without her.

She pulled open her lingerie drawer and slid the letters into a corner, where they joined a small packet of other cards and photos, tied up in a ribbon.

While the drawer was hanging open it was impossible to miss the single pair of white panties perched atop the sea of beige. She smoothed the fine lace between her thumb and forefinger, remembering a night in a secluded school parking lot. Were those panties nothing but a memento of the past now too?

Chapter 32

Esteban tore the GOING OUT OF BUSINESS sign next to his family's market stall out of the ground. Because they'd be back. Next week, and every week after that.

He jerked together the canvas-covered legs of the portable market canopy, impatient to finish cleaning up so he could get to the work that needed doing back home. The canvas felt even heavier than usual this morning, soaked with dew from sitting out overnight. Thankfully, their neighbors at the next stall had crated up all the Moraleses' unsold produce and taken what money was in the till home with them for Esteban to pick up later.

He loaded the unsold food back into the truck. They'd lost a lot of money by having to leave right in the middle of one of the busiest market days of the year. He should be calculating their loss. But all he could think about was Savvy.

He pictured her the day they'd met. So poised behind those black frames. Big contrast between her then, and the way she'd become so flustered in the greenhouse when he'd hidden her glasses. He'd only teased her a minute, but there was no faking that kind of terror. Come to think of it, she'd looked just as scared in the hospital parking lot yesterday. . . .

Angrily, he brushed away any hint of sympathy he might feel for her.

Shane and his gang were right. How had he ever believed there was any way in hell he could be with Sauvignon St. Pierre in the first place?

He grunted as he heaved the heavy canopy into the truck bed, trying awkwardly to maneuver it to where it wouldn't crush everything else.

She was the devil's daughter. Sizzling hot, smart, rich . . . and totally out of his league.

Resting a hand on the edge of the truck bed, he peered around at the deserted stalls. A cumulous cloud passed over the sun, bringing with it a sense of cold, hard reality.

He'd been deluding himself. Trying to grow lavender in clay? Believing for one second that the son of an immigrant truck farmer could be enough for a wine heiress?

He got into the truck, his face hot. He'd been such an idiot. No wonder people had laughed at him.

All that was over now. That was someone else. A man who hadn't yet had his heart ripped out of his chest. Hadn't seen his father collapse onto the pavement in front of half the town, heard his mother's screams. With all that had happened since yesterday, Esteban almost didn't recognize that man anymore.

Jeanne was layering turkey and cheese on a sliced baguette. "I am taking Maria a little lunch. She's spending long hours at the hospital. Maybe you would like to come?"

"I'd love to, after the way I dashed out of the ER yesterday. But I can't. Esteban has banned me from seeing his family."

"Esteban won't be there. He went to the market to collect all their things."

Savvy took a shaky breath, considering. She was dying to see Mrs. Morales.

"Maria asked about you."

"Really?"

Jeanne nodded, smearing her special sauce along the sandwiches. "You would prefer to wander around this big house alone all afternoon?"

"I'm going to the office."

Jeanne scowled. "Today—Sunday?"

"There won't be any distractions there today. No bosses, no phone calls. I need to do some research without anyone looking over my shoulder."

"You could stop at the hospital on the way. It will do both you and Maria good."

When they arrived, Maria Morales stood to welcome them to the cardiac floor's reception room with kisses and hugs.

"He is sleeping," she said softly, as if her husband could hear them.

"Good. You can have a bite while he rests," said Jeanne, handing her a brown bag and a to-go cup of coffee.

"You are so wonderful," said Mrs. Morales, "but I don't think I can eat right now. Would you mind . . . ?"

"Of course! Eat it whenever you like. I made enough for Esteban, also. What are the doctors saying?"

Hooded black eyes darted between Jeanne and Savvy. "The doctor says Geraldo can't work anymore." She wrung her hands. "Esteban says his *padre* can retire and he will do all the work himself. But that's not possible. It's too much for one man alone, even a man as strong as my son. And we can't afford to hire outside help."

"It seems Esteban is making these decisions very quickly. Why not wait a bit, see how Geraldo progresses?

"You know how stubborn he can be. Just like his father." She shook her head. "Such a shame. His lavender plants were finally growing. . . ."

Savvy shrank with remorse and regret.

Mrs. Morales reached for Savvy's hands, layering them between her own. "Don't feel bad," she said. "I always try to encourage Esteban, but it's hard to watch his disappointment these last months, when the rains keep coming and coming. In the end, it's probably for the best that he gives up on his lavender. He does everything he can to fix it, but it's just not the right kind of soil where we live.

"And another thing," she said, squeezing her hands again. "I know you would not lie on purpose. I believe you when you say you didn't know your papa was behind the offers from the beginning."

At least someone did. "Honestly, Mrs. Morales, I feel terrible. I should have known, but I didn't. I would never have believed Papa could stoop so low."

Mrs. Morales took a seat, Jeanne and Savvy flanking her. "Between you and me, I was getting a little excited about those houses at Verdant Acres," she said wistfully. "Fireplaces . . . laundry rooms right off the master bedroom. One whole room, just for the laundry. And the walk-in showers! But then, I think about how much I would miss my *chicas* . . ."

"What will be, will be," said Jeanne soothingly. "For now, you should concentrate on getting your husband better."

"Yes, but then there's the doctor bill, and the hospital. . . . I can't begin to imagine what they will be like. . . ."

An RN carrying a tablet strode briskly down the hall toward the nurse's station.

"There is Sophia, Geraldo's nurse," said Mrs. Morales, rising again, looking after her anxiously. "She's very kind. Explained to me everything when Geraldo was transferred here from the ER. She promised to keep me updated. Maybe she has some news." She kept her eye on the nurses' station, as if hoping for good news could make it materialize.

"I'm going now," Savvy said. "If there's anything I can do for you or Mr. Morales, don't hesitate to call."

"Don't work late," Jeanne said. "You must start taking better care of yourself."

If anyone spotted Savvy going into the office looking the way she did that Sunday afternoon, with the circles under her eyes, sagging ponytail, and boots still dusty from the ranch, he'd think some stranger was breaking in and call the cops, especially if he saw the way she propped her boots on her desk and swiveled back and forth while she pondered her next move.

She looked down at the file labeled NTI/MORALES. Even if all the pieces of that real estate transaction had fallen neatly into place, she would've needed a little hand-holding from one of the partners at closing. After all, Savvy was what was called a "baby lawyer." An apprentice. But now? A transaction *this* complicated was way, way out of her realm.

What was the best outcome for everyone concerned?

She looked down at her hands spanning her flat tummy.

And then she put down her feet, opened her laptop, and started to open tabs.

Cardiac prognoses.

Real estate sales agreements.

Every possible version of legal partnerships. General, limited, LLC, and so on.

For the answers to questions she couldn't find online, she got up and went down the hall to the firm's law library.

She had no idea how many hours she'd spent plowing through the heavy law books and trolling the net before she finally looked up and noticed it was growing dark and she was so hungry she could eat her keyboard.

Monday morning, Esteban hurled the last of the limp Rathmell Ranch lavender plants into the wheelbarrow with the others. Then he wheeled them over to the compost pile. Compost was all they were good for.

He returned to the freshly turned soil and stared blankly down at it. It was still early in the season. Made way more sense to plant that bed in something they could actually make money off of. What had been planted in that spot last year? Right now, he couldn't remember.

Earlier that morning, while Madre was at the hospital, he'd canceled the Realtor appointment for her, rather than put her through the embarrassment of explaining what had happened. Then he'd called up the HR guy at the utility company to tell him he wouldn't be taking that lineman job, after all.

And that was it. Now the only thing left was to finish where Padre had left off with the *Plan Familiar* . . . growing only what thrived on their patch of earth. It wouldn't be easy doing the work of two men, but he was strong. And even if growing vegetables wasn't Esteban's dream, it put food in their mouths and a little money in the bank. Families like the Moraleses didn't have the luxury of chasing rainbows. They'd be fine. He could do this.

He turned and trudged back to the barn to see what seed Padre might have stored up that he could sow right away, before the season got any later.

There was something he *couldn't* do, though, *Plan Familiar* be damned.

Maybe if he had never known Savvy's eager optimism, never held her supple body in his arms, never watched her face contort with pleasure at his touch, he could eventually find someone to settle down with. There were plenty of *chulas* out there.

But now? Seemed like he was fated to take after Uncle in more ways than just his name and his unusual height. Because after Savvy, there could never be anyone else.

The realization left him hollow and listless.

He stared unseeing at the bags of seed Padre had stacked up in the barn. There, in the quiet dimness, where no one could see, he couldn't hold back his hurt any longer.

As he imagined the years stretching out endlessly before him, the tears ran down his face.

Maybe the family's luck would change. Maybe, by some miracle, Esmerelda and Pete would have a son, or one of their daughters would come back here and farm instead of going to college and getting a desk job. At least Padre would be happy.

There would be no sons for Esteban, though.

Así es la vida, he thought. *That's life.*

Chapter 33

"Savvy," Robert Witmer said, glancing up briefly from his laptop. "Come in."

She sat down straight across from him. It was Monday, almost one week since NTI had accepted Geraldo Morales's outrageous counteroffer.

"What can I do for you?" he asked absent-mindedly.

"Did you hear about an incident over the weekend at the opening of the Napa farmers' market?"

"My wife does all the food shopping."

That sounded exactly like something one of Papa's cohorts would say.

"I had to ask. The Morales family has a stall there."

Robert looked up then, his hands freezing on his keyboard. "What sort of incident?"

"Someone informed Esteban Morales that my father was a partner in Napa Terroir Investments."

The skin on Robert's neck above his silk repp tie turned a mottled red.

"And if he were?"

"That would be a problem. Mr. Morales and Papa have never seen eye to eye. I assured Esteban that what he heard wasn't true, but I'll need to take a look at NTI's partnership agreement, to confirm. Would you know where I could find a copy?" Coolly, she glanced around the room.

"I er, uh—" he sputtered.

"Another thing. Can you tell me why an old-boy firm like Witmer, Robinson and Scott hired a young female associate who couldn't care less about golf in the first place?"

Her boss face tried on a variety of expressions while he pondered how to respond.

"Could it have been only as a favor to a friend?"

No wonder Helen and the other assistants had resented Savvy from the get-go.

She got up and crossed Robert's spacious, wood paneled office to the window. "Exactly what kind of a future would said associate have here? I mean, being that she's so, *so* different from all the other partners?"

Her perch on the windowsill gave her a prime view of Robert's bald spot. "Not much, I'm guessing. Now, granted, I'm new at all this. But I always thought the goal of a transactional attorney was to *avoid* litigation, not provoke it. To see into the future of a contract. Scrutinize the language from every party's perspective."

Robert swiveled around to face her. "What are you getting at?"

"I'm trying to keep all our asses out of court."

She rose and walked back to the other side of his desk. He was forced to circle his chair to keep up with her.

"Because right now, the NTI deal is shakier than a subprime mortgage. Esteban Morales is threatening to sue me. And if that happens, guess who I'm going to go after?"

Robert rose from his seat. "Now, look here. There's nothing illegal about—"

"No, you look here." She flattened her palms on his desk and leaned in toward him. "Regardless of whether or not it was illegal to keep me from knowing Papa was involved in a transaction I was tasked with negotiating, there's no question that it was unethical. You used me. Papa used me. Used both of us."

Robert started out from behind his desk. "Ho-hold on. Let's get John and Mike in here. . . . Helen?" He craned his neck around Savvy, directing his voice to his assistant's office across the hall.

"Never mind, Helen," Savvy hollered over her shoulder. "We don't need John and Mike," she told Robert. "I've got it all figured out."

Back at her desk, Savvy punched in a number with a Cupertino area code.

"Hello?"

"Anne? Savvy St. Pierre. Sorry to interrupt your research. I'll get right to the point. I have a proposition for you."

Anne chuckled. "You want me to buy back the still already?"

Savvy smiled for the first time in days. "No, not that. Hear me out. . . ."

"Heard from Papa?" Savvy asked Jeanne that evening, before she even set down her satchel.

Jeanne stretched to put a glass into a tall cupboard. "Not I. You can't reach him?"

"I've called him twice. He must be either tied up"—*ha, poor choice of words*—"or he's avoiding me."

Jeanne's head disappeared below the island as she continued to unload the dishwasher. "Why would he tell me when he's returning? I am merely the *cuisinier* in this house."

"You're way more than the cook, Madame Jeanne, and you know it," Savvy said, pacing between the window and the kitchen island. "I need to talk to him," she muttered, "right after I talk to Mr. Morales."

"Maria is hoping her husband can go home tomorrow or the next day."

Savvy sucked in a breath between her teeth. "That's good news for her. Not for me, though."

"Why not?"

"Once he's discharged, I'll never get to talk to him alone." She bit the inside of her cheek, considering.

"Well then, you had better go and see him soon." Jeanne closed the dishwasher and looked up. "Is there something I can do?"

"Do you speak Spanish?" asked Savvy with a twisted grin.

"You know the answer to that. But maybe there is another way I can help."

Jeanne picked up her phone from the table.

A few minutes later, she filled Savvy in. "Maria is getting ready to go back to Queen of the Valley now, to be with Geraldo over dinner. Visiting hours are over at eight, but she feels very tired this evening, as if this entire incident has finally caught up with her. She doesn't think she will stay all the way 'til the end tonight."

"What about Esteban?"

"Her son was at the hospital this morning. He's back home now. Maria says he has been in the fields until long after dark these past couple of days. Last night he almost fell asleep at the supper table. She's becoming as worried for his health as she is her husband's."

*　*　*

From where she was parked a few rows back, Savvy drummed impatiently on the steering wheel, watching and waiting for Mrs. Morales to step through the sliding glass doors of the hospital. It was after seven when she finally appeared. Savvy recognized her from the weariness in her bearing as much as from her apple shape.

Seven-twenty. Forty minutes until visiting hours ended. Forty minutes to convince a stubborn, sick man to do a complete one-eighty on his philosophy of life—and she didn't even speak his language.

Hopefully, her stint on moot court would come in handy tonight.

She marched down the hallway of the cardiac unit to Mr. Morales's room, one hand on the strap of her satchel containing all the necessary documents—in both English and Spanish. She'd even spelled out her argument and translated that, so she could read it to him. With so many lives at stake, she couldn't just wing it.

She paused in the doorway when she saw Mr. Morales's nurse, Sophia, at his bedside, conversing with him in his native tongue.

"Come in." Sophia smiled in greeting, switching to English. "Tell Señor Morales I'll come back later, when his pretty guest is gone." She turned to leave.

"Actually, would you mind staying? There's something important I need to discuss with him, and I could use your help. My Spanish stinks."

Sophia checked the clock on the wall. "I can stay for a minute or two."

A warm wave of relief washed over Savvy. Not only could Sophia interpret, she would make the perfect witness to the signature Savvy desperately needed to make all of this come together.

After the fight with Esteban last Saturday in the hospital parking lot, Savvy had gone home devastated—and livid. If Papa had been around then, she'd have laid into him without thinking, which would've gotten her exactly nowhere. Now it was Thursday. Waiting all this time to finally confront him was excruciating, but maybe his absence had been a godsend. It had given her time to come up with a plan and set the wheels in motion.

Everything was squared away with her boss, Anne, and Mr. Morales. All she needed now was Papa.

At the office, she bided her time and kept her head down. Papa had to come home eventually.

Then again, Xavier St. Pierre was no typical dad.

Thursday afternoon Savvy's intercom buzzed. "You have a box out here," said Karen.

Savvy sighed. Apparently it was too much trouble for Karen to carry the box down the hall to her. *Oh well.* She wasn't able to concentrate on the dull contract on her desk, anyway. She got up and walked down to the reception area.

The plain cardboard box didn't look like anything special. But when she saw the New York postmark, Savvy remembered.

"Thanks." She smiled politely at Karen.

Once she got into the hallway, she let her face light up. She had to restrain her feet from hurrying. When she reached her office, she closed the door with a soft click, then dashed to her desk to grab the scissors and slit the tape on the package.

Inside she found an envelope.

Ms. St. Pierre, Enclosed are samples of the basic olfactive groups used in perfumery. Please take the time to familiarize yourself with each of these families, studying no more than two groups in any single day. When you feel you have fully internalized them, let me know and we will progress to the next step. Sincerely yours, Lawrence Van Horne.

Savvy tossed the letter aside. Blindly, she thrust a hand into the finely shredded paper and pulled out a brown glass bottle. *Oriental,* said the label. She dug back in. *Citrus.* Next was *Woody.* Then came *Aromatic, Floral,* and *Chypre.*

She cradled each of the cool bottles in her palm, turning it around and around until the heat from her body warmed it. She was dying to open every single one of them, to inhale their magic, learn their secrets.

With a tug of regret, she carefully packed them up again, replaced the letter in its envelope on the top, and folded in the flaps to keep the contents safe.

The day would come when she could trust her sense of smell again. Until then, she would have to be patient.

She tried Papa's phone once more. Nothing. Dropping her phone to her desk with a clatter, she propped her head with her hand and gazed at the papers strewn across her desk. She was behind schedule. She'd have to stay late.

At six-thirty, her phone rang.

"Mademoiselle? Your papa, he is home."

"Papa?"

Savvy stormed into the house, popping her head into one after another of the rooms off the foyer.

"Papa!" Her voice sounded strident to her ears.

Char appeared over the second-floor balustrade with a look of concern. "Savvy?"

"Where is he?"

"Have you checked the lab?"

Savvy turned to go back outside, to the building that housed the blending lab. "If you see him"—she pointed up at Char—"don't let him leave."

Outside, she swept down the curved staircase and took off to where the outbuildings sat, great black rectangles in a darkening sky. Sure enough, there was a light on, over in the lab. The minute it took to march out there was enough to regenerate the full head of steam that she'd had to suppress for the past six days.

"Sauvignon!" Papa looked up from where he held what looked like a skinny turkey baster, piping jewel-red liquids—cabernet, merlot and other varietals—from their graduated cylinders into a wineglass. *"Ça va?"*

In her fury, the lab aromas of cherry, tobacco, and licorice that usually piqued her interest barely registered.

"Never mind how I am. Why didn't you tell me?"

"Tell you what, *chèrie?"*

"You know what! The Morales land! NTI!"

"Ah. You know."

"Agggh!" She put her hands to her head. "Did you actually think you could get away with this?"

"You could have asked to see the partnership agreement at any time."

"Why should I do that when I assumed everything was on the level? That the only person I needed to deal with was Don Smith—the general partner, the decision maker? Why should I even have considered that you might be involved? I suppose that's one of the reasons you picked me to do your dirty work, huh? Because I was so inexperienced?"

Papa rose from the table. Before his next words left his lips, Savvy moved in on him.

"And now I find out Smith is nothing but a straw buyer, and you're the real one! You're Napa Terroir Investors! Only you! Tell me this, Papa. Did you cook this up before you even got Robert to hire me?"

His guilty face said it all.

She began to stalk him. "Of all the things you've ever done," she said, struggling to maintain her composure. "Forcing me to bail you out of jail . . . running around with women younger than Meri, for God's sake." She rolled her eyes and shook her head. "Not coming home for Christmas last year after you *promised* us. . . . Do I have to go on?"

His cocky smile wavered.

"This is the *worst.*" He flinched when she poked his chest. "Everyone in this valley knew you were behind that land grab except me. How is that? How does that even *happen*?" She stabbed him again, harder.

He inched backward as she trailed him around the lab.

"Do you know what you've done?"

His hand went down on the edge of a sink to steady himself, sending a glass pipette crashing brittle-y to the floor.

Savvy barely blinked. "Your sleazy underhandedness has cost you this deal. And it's cost me the man I love!"

"Ah!" He brightened. "You *did* sleep with Esteban Morales!"

Savvy steamed. "Yes! I slept with him! And I'll admit, my motives were selfish, in the beginning. Then I got to know Esteban and his family. I've never met more noble, self-effacing people than the Moraleses. They live for each other, not only themselves. Imagine that, Papa!"

"It is possible to sleep with a man without falling in love with him."

"Don't give me your damn French platitudes!" She swung away, sickened by the sight of him. "You really don't get it, do you? I fell in love with Esteban because of his goodness, not to get something out of him. Leave it to you to twist things around!"

Gingerly, he approached her back. "*Chèrie.* Esteban Morales is a poor truck farmer. He is no one to become distraught over."

Savvy pressed her lips together, her self-control unraveling like a pulled sweater.

"He is nothing but an immigrant."

She whirled around. "Seriously? Esteban speaks better English than you do, even though you were born here!"

"Calm down, *ma chère*. We will fix this."

"Uh, no. *We* won't fix this. *I* will fix it. And I'm going to tell you how.

"*Vraiment?*" He lifted a brow.

"Yes, really. You're going to do exactly what I tell you to do."

His confident smirk faded. "Or what?"

"I'll tell you what," she snarled. "Now, sit down."

Chapter 34

I need you.

That's what the text said. Not *I need to talk to you, I need to see you*, or any variation of that. Just *I need you*.

Cristo. Why now?

Padre was back home where he belonged. He was a couch jockey nowadays, not toiling next to Esteban in the garden. Madre hovered over him like a hyperactive honeybee. At least that kept her off Esteban's case about how hard he was pushing himself.

Padre's mood was surprisingly chipper. Esteban could hardly believe how accepting he was of his diagnosis. The day he'd come home from the hospital, he'd given his son an awkward one-armed hug and told him how proud he was of him. Maybe having a heart attack had done something to the wiring in his brain.

Esteban had too much on his mind already to wonder what had gotten into Padre.

George had given Esteban some flak about reneging on the lineman job after he'd put himself out there for him. Esteban didn't blame him, but what else could he do? He was needed here, at home.

Bottom line, though, was that as hard as the St. Pierres had tried to screw up everyone's lives, they'd failed. All that was in the past. Now all the Morales family felt was relief that Padre was out of danger. They were settling into their new normal: Padre guarding his fragile health, Madre caring for him, and Esteban only coming in from the fields to eat and sleep. Doing what any son would do for his family.

The last thing he needed right now was a cryptic text from a wine heiress. He deleted her words, rejecting the pounding of his heart. But the second he shoved his phone back in his jeans it pinged again.

Meet me tomorrow, 10am, Rathmell Ranch.

The next morning he found himself driving up the steep grade to the ranch, kicking himself all the way.

Dios, though, it was gorgeous up here. That, he couldn't deny.

There was Savvy's black Mercedes, sitting at the top of the hill.

He parked his Chevy and set out for the distillery, betting he'd find her there. But before he'd gotten far, his peripheral vision caught a figure standing like a sunflower in thigh-high Hidcote with her back to him.

Out there in that deserted field, the high altitude breeze rippled the folds of a pale pink dress around narrow hips. A feminine hand smoothed back loose strands of long chestnut hair. When he got to within thirty feet of her, she slowly turned, somehow sensing his silent presence. Gone were the ugly glasses. Her naked gaze pierced him like an arrow, taking his breath away.

His legs got a mind of their own, carrying him forward until they were close enough to talk.

"You came."

He'd been right before. No one could compare with Savvy.

Still, a man had his pride.

"Why'd you call me out here?"

"How's your father?"

"Fine." Esteban kicked the dry, crumbly dirt—the kind of dirt he dreamed about—with the toe of his boot. "Better than fine. He's . . . I don't know. Different."

"He didn't tell you, then. I thought he might," she murmured.

"Tell me what?" He knew this would be a mistake. Now what had she done?

"Do you like it here, Esteban?" she asked, peering out at the distant, rolling hills.

Dios. His name on her lips took him back to parked cars and a sandy beach. His gaze followed hers over the house with the orange tile roof, the peach orchard, the scrub-covered ridges.

Of course he liked it here. He raised a hand like *duh*, and uttered a guttural noise of agreement.

"I mean, do you *like* it, like it?"

"Dammit, Savvy, I don't have time for your prima donna games. I got work to do...." He turned to start back to his truck. If he left right now, he'd only have lost an hour of daylight.

"Wait..." Her hand appealed to him. "There's so much I have to tell you...."

Suddenly the anger he hadn't known he'd been stuffing down for the past week while he juggled problems of life and death sprang to the surface. "Then tell me! You can start with explaining how I'm supposed to believe you and your old man weren't in cahoots together since the very first day we met!"

She took a step toward him. "Papa planned this months ago. First, he got his pal Robert Witmer to hire me. Then he used Don Smith as his cover to buy your land. Papa asked Robert to have me handle the deal, in part because I was so green. He was banking on me not digging into the NTI partnership agreement."

Esteban felt his blood simmer to the point of boiling—but not because of anything Savvy had done. Could this be true? *Her own father?* What was worse, St. Pierre had to know Savvy would be irresistible to a man like him. Hell, to any man. *Still...* "How can I believe you?"

"Robert signed an affidavit admitting he never clued me in on the real identity of NTI. I have it with me, in the car. I'll show you."

Esteban huffed. "One lawyer sticking up for another lawyer? That's it? That's all you've got?"

"Esteban—"

"You told me yourself that the most important thing to you in life was getting ahead in your career. Making partner."

"It was. But I never told you why." She took some worn paper rectangles from her pocket and handed them out. "The thing I've always cared about the most, the thing that kept me motivated since I was twelve years old, was taking care of my sisters."

He refused to take the notes from her hand. "What do they need you for? You said they were doing great. Got good jobs... isn't one of them engaged?"

"They're doing great now, but there was a time when they depended on me, and I couldn't help them. That affected me more than I could ever explain." She nodded toward the notes. "Read them. Please."

He skimmed over the contents of one of them, then lowered it to his side. "What about us? Were you faking liking me? For my land?"

Savvy huffed softly, looking him up and down. "I'm a lawyer, not an actress." Then she averted her gaze. "I'll admit it, though. When the deal was falling apart, I thought sleeping with you might reignite it."

He felt his heart harden and his molars clench.

"I had it all planned out. Bought a new dress, new underwear, CVS's entire stock of condoms. . . ."

He frowned, remembering. "That day at the beach. *That* underwear was for me?"

She blushed. "That was my work underwear. It wasn't supposed to happen that day. Remember? You invited me along at the last minute. The first time was supposed to be the night after I took you to that shop in downtown Napa. Those white lace panties? Those were for you.

"That day on the beach was totally spontaneous—in every way. I didn't fake anything. You were the first." She edged closer, bringing with her the scent of roses. "I swear on my mother's grave. If you don't believe anything else, believe that."

How did she do that? Take him from gutted to on top of the world with a wave of her wand?

She stepped up until she stood in front of him. "Your father signed a new contract to sell."

Wha—?

"I reworked the sales agreement it so that your parents can lease back the house and land for the remainder their lifetimes. Everything about the farm will look the same as it always has. They'll live out their lives in the home they love, in exchange for a small monthly leaseback fee that they'll barely notice coming out of their bank account. The only thing different is they'll clear two million dollars from the sale, so they won't have to work. If they choose to continue to farm, they can hire help."

"How's that help Xavier?"

"The land will eventually be planted in winegrapes, after your parents are gone. That's the compromise."

When he recovered his shock, he said, "And you'll get a sweet little commission. What're you going to do with that?"

"Use it as a down payment."

"On what?"

"This." Savvy spread her arms. "It wasn't working out here for Anne and Lucas. They're more city than country mice, they decided. They were thrilled to entertain my offer."

His brows knit. "You're not a farmer. You have no clue what you're doing."

"I want to make perfume. People change and grow, Esteban, like plants. Dreams change. Sometimes they die—"

"Sometimes they get killed," Esteban interjected.

She smiled wistfully. "I realized I was doing something I didn't really enjoy, for reasons that no longer applied. You're right. Char and Meri don't need me anymore. Everyone could see that except me. Now, Papa . . . I can't even. God knows I've already bailed him out enough times. That man was born trouble.

"I could open a solo practice, work out of the farmhouse here. Haven't decided yet. It depends."

"Depends on what?"

She turned and stood next to him so that they were gazing out at the same view. "You're right. I'm in way over my head here. I need someone who knows what he's doing. Someone with strength and experience." She took his hand. "Come with me. Be my partner. We'll make our dreams come true, together."

"And let you support me? No." He looked down, shaking his head. "No way."

"We'll be equal partners. Your father has offered to give you— *lend*, if you insist—as much money as you need. Everything else is right here. You could make this the most amazing lavender farm in California."

He yearned to trust her, but after all that had happened . . .

"How did you get our fathers to agree to all this?"

"Your father wants you to be happy."

"There's more to it than that. How'd you get them to come to terms? They hate each other!"

She faced him again, taking one of his hands in each of hers. "I told them that was the only way they'd get to see their first grandson."

He stared slack-jawed at her face, then her belly. A shiver ran up his spine.

"I've prepared documents stating that when your parents are gone, the title to their farm will pass directly into our child's name. Along

with his rightful portion of all the other Domaine St. Pierre properties, of course."

The *Plan Familiar.* She'd thought of everything.

"If you say no, I can raise our baby at the winery. Continue at the
same law firm, hire a nanny. . . ."

But Esteban wasn't hearing a word she said.

"*Woot!*" he hollered. Savvy squealed as he scooped her into his arms
and twirled her around in the fertile field. *"Woo hoo hoo hoo hoo!"*

Chapter 35

"Get up! Get up!"

Savvy's mattress rocked and swayed. Her eyes flew open. *Was it the Big One?*

No. These voices weren't panicky. They sounded—exuberant.

"Get up!" Her sisters' voices.

She sat bolt upright. Sometimes she still forgot she wasn't Meri and Char's protector anymore, after having assigned herself that role for so long.

"Happy wedding day! Happy wedding day!" The girls bounded onto her king-sized bed.

Savvy sighed with relief and sank back down into the cozy warmth of her covers. "What time is it?" she croaked.

The mattress jolted violently again. "Time to get up!"

A deep-chested *ooof* was followed by a shriek and a body boomeranging away.

"What's *he* doing here?"

Savvy opened one eye to see Meri pointing at the other side of the bed. All the ruckus hadn't so much as budged Esteban.

"No fair. That's breaking the rules," scolded Char, climbing off, too. "The groom's not supposed to spend the night before your wedding with you. It's bad luck."

"And now we know why. Liable to get kneed in the kidney," grumbled Esteban, his voice muffled in his pillow.

"Leave us alone," Savvy groaned, snuggling deeper. "Is it even light out yet?" Hadn't last night's rehearsal dinner, highlighted by Jeanne and Mrs. Morales congratulating each other, just ended? She heard the scrape of drapery rings being drawn across their metal rod, saw the brightness seeping in behind closed lids.

"It's eleven o'clock!" sang Meri. "You're getting married in exactly seven hours!"

From that moment on, Savvy's day was a whirlwind of hair and makeup and a gaggle of strong-willed women telling her to stay calm and at the same time making her a basket case.

Finally, it was time for her to be squeezed into "the dress." What a shopping ordeal that had been! There'd been way too many opinions to consider. Meri had pressed for something edgy and low cut. Jeanne had said her wedding gown must be simple and chic. And Mrs. Morales had been a fan of a getup that made Savvy feel as if she were nine feet wide and drowning in a sea of Spanish lace. Of course, Char had advised Savvy not to listen to anyone except herself.

She spread her fingers along her thickening waistline and peered down at the creamy swath of fabric crisscrossing her bosom. Amazing what a bun in the oven could do for your boobage.

"It is time," said Jeanne, eyes twinkling. "Look at you." She held her at arm's length. "A June bride. At the beginning of this year, who would have believed you would be married before your sisters? You were wise to take my advice concerning the dress. You are a vision."

"Aw, Jeanne, thank you for helping me pick it out." Savvy reached out to hug her.

"*Non non non non non, mademoiselle.*" Jeanne touched her balled up hanky to her nose, her brow crinkled. "That is the last time I may call you that." She paused to contain her emotions, then lifted her chin "It would not be good to muss your hair." She kissed the air around Savvy's cheeks.

Savvy gathered up her skirt, surprised at how much silk jersey could weigh. Then Jeanne helped her down the staircase, and together they wound through the house to where Papa was supposed to be waiting in the covered portico by the pool to walk her down the aisle.

But when they got there, Papa was nowhere to be found.

"What time is it now?" Esteban asked George out of the corner of his mouth. He ran a finger between his neck and the stifling collar of his shirt. *Mierda,* it was hot out. June had been as dry as the winter had been wet. The lavender at the ranch was going great guns.

The wedding party had been hanging around the pool, out of sight of the guests, for what seemed like an eternity.

George checked his watch yet again. "Six-twenty-nine."

The ceremony was to have started at six.

"He'll be here. You kidding me? After spending half a fortune on this clambake? Trust me. He'll be here."

If George wasn't worried, why had he sent Tomas off to hunt for Xavier a half hour ago?

Across the portico, Savvy's attendants hovered over her, but between them Esteban could see the worry etched in her face. It wasn't good for her to be standing like that for so long in her condition. Even he knew that.

He was going over there. He couldn't bear to see her suffer for one more minute.

When her concerned sisters saw him coming, they stepped back to let him in. No one chastised him now for breaking the rule of not seeing the bride before the ceremony.

"Let's walk," he said, giving Savvy his arm.

She turned in the direction of the lawn where their vows were scheduled to take place.

But he didn't budge. Char's sisters had pleaded with them not to peek at the grounds ahead of time. Their father had had people out there working nonstop for the past week, spiffing it up for the ceremony. "You'll spoil the surprise," Esteban said. But that wasn't the real reason he kept her away. Seeing all their guests milling about there, waiting and wondering what the hold up was, might only make her feel worse. "Other way."

"No. I want to see what it looks like."

Now Savvy peeked around a column, gasped, and put her fingers to her lips. "Oh."

From behind her, Esteban peered over her head to see for himself.

They faced the back of the crowd and the entrance to a long, grassy aisle sprinkled thickly with yellow rose petals. A gold satin ribbon—a flimsy barrier restricting all but the wedding party from the path leading between rows of gilded chairs—had been tied between pillars topped with urns, overflowing with more roses. The aisle ended at a sweep of curved pergola dripping with wisteria and Spanish moss. In the center, a wine barrel served as an altar. Off to one side, a string quartet played a classical air for the throng of well-dressed people sipping wine, nibbling hors d'oeuvres.

The violet Mayacamas presided in the distance, echoing the color of the flowers.

"Did you have a hand in any of this?" Esteban asked.

Savvy shook her head, unable to look away. "If I'd had it my way, it'd just be you and me, up at the ranch. It was all Papa. He wanted to throw us a party."

Party? Ha. This was St. Pierre's attempt to buy back Savvy's good graces, after all he'd put her through.

"*Mierda*." Esteban reached around to cup Savvy's belly. "You didn't hear that," he said to the four-month bump.

Those people have been waiting a mighty long time, he thought. The guests had had no idea the private event they'd been asked to attend was a wedding. There'd been no save-the-dates, not even a written invitation. Nothing that would be a red flag to the media.

Savvy turned toward Esteban. The mask of calm she fought to keep on her face didn't fool him one minute.

"Come on. Let's go back," he said.

Minutes later, back in the portico, Tomas dashed up to the couple and George. "His helicopter just left SFO."

"Won't be long now," said George. "It's only about a twenty-minute flight up from the city."

Esteban tried to get a read on Savvy.

With a diamond-clad finger, she flicked away a single tear. "We were supposed to have been walking down the aisle forty minutes ago, and he just took off?" She lowered her gaze to the patio, lips quivering.

Don't cry, Savvy. Her old man had already been on her last nerve, and now this. The one thing Esteban couldn't handle was if she cried sad tears on her wedding day. Anything she wanted, he would do. He felt his fists bunch, imagining the ways he wanted to make Xavier St. Pierre pay for causing the woman he loved so much pain. *Please don't cry.*

Savvy didn't cry. As soon as she'd regained her composure she looked up, cleared her throat, and pasted on a bright smile. "Cue the music," she said, looking to George and Tomas and her sisters to lead the procession.

To the amplified notes of George Winston's "Joy" from a baby grand, the crowd came to its feet. Esteban waited while Meri and George, then Char and Tomas paraded down the aisle. At the altar, they stopped, the girls clutching their bouquets, smiling prettily across from George and Tomas.

He looked lovingly at his bride, carrying his son inside her.

Padre was right. The Lord works in mysterious ways.

He offered her his arm.

"Let's go." She gazed up at him and together they stepped out onto rose petals, and it became a blur of three hundred smiling faces smiling back at them . . . Savvy handing off her bouquet to Char . . . the homily and the songs and the prayers . . . and then, while Madre wept tears of happiness and Padre's chest puffed out like a pigeon's, Sauvignon St. Pierre gave Esteban something greater than even his Michoacán grandfather could have dreamed of.

Love the Napa Wine Heiresses?
Then keep reading for a glimpse at
The most shocking event in their lives yet!
A TASTE OF SAKE
Available Fall 2015

And be sure to check out
A TASTE OF CHARDONNAY
And
A TASTE OF MERLOT
Available now

Chapter 1

The farm boy and the heiress. That was the phrase whispered among the out-of-towners during the long wait for the ceremony to begin.

And that's exactly what it looked like on the surface as Esteban Morales, deltoids threatening to bust out of his shoulder seams, led Sauvignon St. Pierre, the epitome of elegance with her auburn hair pulled back to accent her oval face, down the grassy aisle toward a pergola dripping with wisteria where they were to make their vows.

The reality was a little more complicated. True, the bride had been born into one of California's wealthiest wine families. But when it came to substance . . . character . . . call it what you will—the immigrant Morales truck farmers had it all over the St. Pierre dynasty. Every Napan here knew it, but not one dared utter it out loud.

Last month when Bill Diamond got the phone call inviting him to the Domaine St. Pierre estate on this late June afternoon, he had no idea what this chagigah was all about. He figured it was one of Xavier St. Pierre's summer galas . . . a high point of the social calendar. As sometime real estate agent to Chardonnay and Merlot St. Pierre, Bill was pleasantly surprised to find he'd made the guest list.

Then to find out that this was a wedding—and of St. Pierre's oldest daughter, no less? Even cooler. Bill didn't even mind the delay in the start of the ceremony. How could anyone complain, when St. Pierre kept the wine flowing freely? Bill passed the time making new acquaintances. No such thing as a shy, successful Realtor.

St. Pierre knew how to throw a party, that's for sure. Star-studded crowd—*was that a Mondavi over there?*—flowers everywhere you looked. Live music and butlered hors d'oeuvres passed even before the ceremony got underway. Beneath the pergola, a wine barrel served as a makeshift altar. Then again, what would you expect from Xavier St. Pierre but a blatant tribute to Dionysus? The god of wine had been good to him. *Very* good.

Bill was seated in the second row on the bride's side of the aisle. The lady with the big pink hat in the front row must be a close family friend. St. Pierre's wife was gone, killed years ago in a car accident. Every time Bill heard the barely disguised envy in the valley folks' muttering that the St. Pierre heiresses had it all, it stirred up a rogue urge to rush to their defense. Those people seemed to conveniently forget the SPs had been raised without a mom's loving hand. Bill Diamond couldn't imagine anything worse than growing up motherless.

But where was Xavier?

The wedding party was in position, the music stopped. Three of the string quartet tucked their instruments under their arms and the cellist slid his left hand down the neck of his cello, his bow hand coming to rest on his knee.

The priest waited pointedly for the guests to quiet, then put on a practiced smile and said to the couple, "Please hold hands."

Game time. So why wasn't Savvy mooning back at Esteban during this pivotal moment? Why was she peering out into the distance, her smooth brow pinched with concern?

A faint *chug-chug-chug* entered Bill's consciousness. Damn leaf blowers. He realized he'd filtered the engine sound out until that moment, to focus on the spectacle in front of him. Some of the ritzier neighborhoods were enacting bans on lawn machines on certain days. He was all for that.

But that was no leaf blower. This sound was coming from overhead. That's when he saw the chopper, the size of an acorn, coming up from the south.

No big deal. Any second its course would take it veering away.

But as the seconds rat-a-tat-tatted by, instead of heading away the helo seemed to be making a beeline for the winery. When even the groom glanced around to look, polite twittering rippled through the crowd.

The racket grew, eclipsing the sermon. Bill only caught every other word, ". . . love . . . trust . . . marriage a sacred oath . . ."

Undaunted, the priest cranked up the volume. "Esteban Morales, do you take this woman to be your lawful wedded wife, to have and to hold—"

"I do," Esteban broke in, loud and clear. Following another backward glance, Esteban's right foot turned almost imperceptibly in the direction of the sheltering mansion.

Bill kept a discreet eye on the sky while around him the murmuring swelled into nervous laughter. A head turned here, a chin pointed there. Something about the chopper's trajectory didn't seem right. It wasn't flying in a straight line, or at a consistent altitude. It swung from side to side, rising and falling at random. Among the crowd, the tension built like a storm.

"Sauvignon St. Pierre, do you take this man to be your lawfully wedded hus—"

"I do." Bill read her lips.

The helicopter drew closer and closer, larger and larger, a big-eyed bug. Christ, why was it rocking like that—as if the pilot were drunk at the controls?

A chill went up Bill's spine. Was he actually going to bring it down here? Right here, in the middle of the wedding?

The tall cypress trees surrounding the estate began to sway and pitch. Looking skyward, the priest raised his voice as loud as he could without letting panic seep in. "ThenbythepowervestedinmebytheChurchofAlmightyGodandtheStateofCaliforniaIherebypronouceyoumanandwife. *Run!*"

The groom grabbed his bride's arm and tugged her toward the protection of the house, but Savvy's feet were rooted to the grass, her mouth hanging open in horror. Not wasting a second, he swept her up—a piece of cake for a man of his size—and took off at a tear.

"Go!" shouted Bill, hand on the back of the man standing next to him. Women screamed and men yelled under the now-deafening machine-gun drone of the chopper.

"He's coming down!"

"Get out of the way!"

Chairs toppled like bowling pins. The heavy woman seated next to Bill was knocked to the ground. He stopped and yanked her up by the arm.

"He's not going to make it!" somebody cried.

"Get up!" yelled Bill to the woman. *"Come on!"*

The woman panted, wincing in pain. *"I can't! My ankle!"*

Thanks only to the adrenaline rushing through his body, he hauled her to her feet. "Put your arm around my waist!" Burdening himself with her was going to be the death of him, but he couldn't just run away and leave her to burn up in the imminent fireball.

"It's going to crash!" said the lady in a wobbly voice, some perverted fascination making her look back, slowing them up even more.

Bill jerked her onward toward an outbuilding. "Keep going! Don't look back!"

This was happening.

Bill managed to get her around the back of the shed, where she melted onto the grass. It wasn't much in the way of shelter, but it was better than nothing. Ignoring his own advice, he peered around the corner. Directly above the altar, the helicopter's engine sputtered, died, revived and sputtered again. It shuddered and swung in midair for a surreal moment, like a puppet on a string.

How is that even possible?

Tucking back, Bill crouched and covered his head with his arms, steeling himself for the impact.

There was a dull thud, a sharp crack. The earth shook beneath his feet.

Next to him, the woman whimpered.

And then there was only the sound of the cypress branches, swooshing softly back into place.

Bill peeked around the corner of the shed. The lawn was in shambles. Chairs upended, a portion of the pergola sagging all the way to the ground, floral arrangements broken apart and scattered. In the middle of it all sat the helicopter, leaning sharply to the left.

The rotors were still. There was no smoke, no fire. No twisted metal. From somewhere in the distance came a faint sob. From somewhere else, a masculine voice intoned, "Call 911."

Gradually, the surroundings came back to life. Guests crept tentatively out of the far corners of the winery grounds and buildings, brushing themselves off, retrieving lost hats and heels.

Esteban Morales sprinted from the mansion to the crash site, followed by his wife, who ignored his shouted pleas to stay back.

Merlot dashed out of the building housing the blending lab, into the arms of her relieved boyfriend.

"You okay?" Bill asked the trembling woman next to him. At her nod, he jogged toward the wreckage to see if he could be of assistance.

The chopper's right landing skid lay some distance away, snapped off in the impact, which explained why the cabin was leaning so hard. But wait—there was movement behind the reflective windscreen. The pilot's door cracked open.

Out on Dry Creek Road, a siren wailed.

And then, out climbed Xavier St. Pierre. He ducked beneath the blades and zipped around the front of the chopper to the other side.

"Bon après-midi!" he called, waving to Bill and the stunned semi-circle fast accumulating, as if wrecking a small aircraft in the midst of a wedding was all in a day's work.

He yanked on his passenger's door. Its bottom edge ripped into the lawn, building a dam of dirt. Using both hands, he yanked again.

Bill gestured to the others. "C'mon, help me prop it up." He and a couple of the other younger men pushed the chopper upright, holding it there until Xavier got the door open.

Face first onto the lawn fell a female passenger. Long black hair spread out over her shoulders onto the grass. She didn't move, didn't utter a sound.

Carefully, the men set the chopper back down.

The bride and her sisters ventured closer to the victim. Everyone knew St. Pierre was a player. Was this his latest fling? The poor girl lay there, unmoving. Was she hurt?

Bill knelt next to her, then turned to the rubberneckers. "Is there a doctor here? A nurse?" he called. Now would be a good time for someone to step up. But all he saw was a wall of St. Pierre's cronies—vintners, politicians, entertainers—staring back at him. None of them was any better equipped than a Realtor when it came to caring for a helicopter crash victim.

His gaze swung back to the person on the ground.

"Don't touch her," yelled a woman on the fringe, cell phone glued to her ear. "There's an ambulance on its way."

Gently, Bill lifted the girl's hair from her face. "Are you okay?"

Just then a terrier-like object flew out of the helicopter, scrabbling up next to the girl. It barred its teeth and growled, revealing a prominent underbite.

Bill held out a hand for the dog to sniff. "Easy, boy."

The dog whined, licked his chops, and panted.

"Hang tight. Help's on the way."

Unceremoniously, St. Pierre reached between Bill and the passenger and pulled her up by the hand. "She is not hurt."

Once she was on her feet, Bill saw that she was no girl. No mistaking that. Her silhouette went in and out, not straight up and down. Beneath thick dark brows were slanted eyelids. Her brown eyes projected terror, but she wasn't bleeding and everything looked like it worked. The only visible evidence of her ordeal was a grass stain on her cheek and the yellow rose petals stuck to her dress—if you could call it that. This dress was so short, it was more like a top.

The dog ran a joyful circle around her. St. Pierre slung an arm across her shoulders.

"Sauvignon? Chardonnay? Merlot?"

Savvy and her sisters stared, dumbstruck.

Just behind them, all was silent. The only thing stirring was the gentle billowing of the bridesmaid's full skirts. Everyone wanted to be able to say later that they had heard the first words out of Xavier St. Pierre's mouth after he crash-landed smack into his eldest daughter's wedding.

"I present to you your half sister, Sake."

Heather Heyford learned to walk and talk in Texas, then moved to England. *("Y'all want some scones?")* While in Europe, Heather was forced by her cruel parents to spend Saturdays in the leopard-print vinyl back seat of their Peugeot, motoring from one medieval pile to the next for the lame purpose of "learning something." What she soon learned was how to allay the boredom by stashing a *Cosmo* under the seat. Now a recovering teacher, Heather writes romance, feeds hard-boiled eggs to suburban foxes, and makes art in the Mid-Atlantic. She is represented by the Nancy Yost Literary Agency.

www.ingramcontent.com/pod-product-compliance
Lightning Source LLC
Chambersburg PA
CBHW031420250626
47155CB00004B/1567